**The rumble grew louder, turning into a loud roar. He shifted his gaze back to The Lodge, and the sight that greeted him turned his guts to water.**

A massive wall of snow was racing down the mountain, gaining speed as it moved. The tsunami of white rose up, seeming to dwarf the gondola as it hung precariously above the chaos below.

"Oh my God." Molly gripped him so tightly her nails dug into his skin, even through the fabric of his sweater.

The slight stinging pain snapped Max out of his shock. "It's okay," he said automatically.

"How can you say that?" Molly's voice trembled.

Because he wanted to protect her. He wanted to stand between her and the wall of snow and ice threatening to bury them.

But he was powerless against the forces of nature. And they both knew it.

\* \* \*

**The Coltons of Roaring Springs:
Family and true love are under siege**

\* \* \*

If you're on Twitter, tell us what you think se!

Dear Reader,

It's always so much fun for me to write a book set in the world of the Coltons. This huge family feels like a group of old friends to me now, and I love to explore the emotional connections between these characters as they overcome the challenges in their lives.

Max and Molly are two of the lucky ones—they share a once-in-a-lifetime connection, the kind of bond neither one of them can deny. But when a major misunderstanding threatens to pull them apart, they both have to make a choice: fight through the pain or walk away to nurse their broken hearts alone. But can they survive without each other? And now that Molly is pregnant, should they even try?

This is an emotional story. Molly and Max are forced to navigate loss, grief and danger, all while trying to figure out what the future holds for them. Will they become a family? Or will their problems prove too great an obstacle to overcome? I hope you'll enjoy finding out!

Happy reading!

*Lara*

# COLTON'S COVERT BABY

---

**Lara Lacombe**

⟨H⟩ HARLEQUIN® ROMANTIC SUSPENSE

Special thanks and acknowledgment are given to Lara Lacombe for her contribution to The Coltons of Roaring Springs miniseries.

ISBN-13: 978-1-335-66201-9

Colton's Covert Baby

Copyright © 2019 by Harlequin Books S.A.

Recycling programs for this product may not exist in your area.

**Printed in U.S.A.**

www.Harlequin.com

**Lara Lacombe** earned a PhD in microbiology and immunology and worked in several labs across the country before moving into the classroom. Her day job as a college science professor gives her time to pursue her other love—writing fast-paced romantic suspense with smart, nerdy heroines and dangerously attractive heroes. She loves to hear from readers! Find her on the web or contact her at laralacombewriter@gmail.com.

Visit the Author Profile page at Harlequin.com for more titles.

For A.B. and A.M.—love you both!

# Chapter 1

*I'm not going to make it.*

Molly Gilford walked quickly through the main floor of The Lodge, headed for the gondola dock at the back of the massive structure. As the only five-star resort located on Pine Peak, The Lodge catered to guests who enjoyed winter sports. Skiing, snowboarding, hiking, even camping—the outdoor activities were designed for every skill level, from beginner to expert. And when the guests were done playing in the snow, they came inside to enjoy all the luxuries The Lodge had to offer.

As director of guest services, Molly couldn't help but view the space with a critical eye, even as she dashed past. There was snow packed into the weave of the mat by the main entrance, tracked in by guests and staff alike. A few discarded coffee cups sat on a table in one of the many conversation nooks arranged throughout the room. One of the curtains was askew, and was that a…nose print on the window? Molly squinted, pausing in her journey. Yes, it looked like the glass bore a smudge from what was likely a dog's nose, given its location on the window and the extent of the smear. She shook her head and set off again, her low heels sounding out a rapid tattoo on the pale gray marble tiles. Overall, not a bad state of affairs, but not up to the lofty standards of The Lodge, either.

She took her phone out of her purse as she stepped into the gondola carriage, typing out her observations in a message to the head of housekeeping. Nadia Carrington was Molly's right-hand woman, and she knew the older lady would ensure that the small issues Molly had noticed would be addressed within minutes.

That task done, she checked the time. Two fifty-seven. Three minutes until departure. She'd meant to take the ride down the mountain an hour ago, but time had gotten away from her. There was nothing to do about it now. Her doctor's appointment was at three thirty. It took fifteen minutes to ride down, giving her the same amount of time to find her car and make the drive into town. She was going to be late for certain, but hopefully the same could be said for Dr. Allen, who offered Sunday appointments once a month as a courtesy to her patients.

With nothing to do but wait, Molly glanced

around the interior of the gondola carriage. It was a large space, big enough to hold twenty people at a time. A few small tables and chairs were arranged along the curve of the glass wall at the front of the carriage, which maximized the view for guests as they glided down the mountain. The soft gray carpet and matching drapes ensured that the interior of the gondola did nothing to distract from the scenery— if you stood at the front of the carriage, with the sky above you and the snowy slopes below, it was easy to imagine you were floating down the mountain.

Molly had the carriage to herself, which wasn't too surprising. At this time of day, most guests were either enjoying the outdoors or staying inside to pamper themselves at the spa. Traffic would pick up again in the evening as guests from The Lodge made their way to The Chateau or the town beyond for dinner.

There was a small refrigerator next to the gondola entrance. Molly retrieved a bottle of water and sank onto the seat of a chair. It felt good to get off her feet, if only for the short ride.

She rubbed her hand absently over her belly, anticipation building in her chest as her thoughts turned to her upcoming appointment. It was time for the twenty-week sonogram, when the doctor would do a thorough exam of the baby to make sure everything looked as it should. She'd been excited about this date for months, imagining what her baby might look like. She couldn't wait to see the little hands and feet, hear the steady *thump* of the heartbeat. And perhaps most exciting of all, today she would learn if she was having a girl or a boy.

Molly smiled to herself, warmth blooming inside her as she considered each possibility. Of course, a healthy baby was her top priority, but she had to admit, she was kind of hoping for a girl. Boys grew up and left their mothers behind, whereas girls were better at staying connected to family. Her own situation was a perfect example—if not for her reminders, Molly's brother, Mason, would never remember to call their mother on her birthday or send their dad a Father's Day card. She and her younger sister, Sabrina, were the ones who kept in regular contact with their parents.

"I hope you'll do the same," she said softly to her baby. She couldn't bear the thought of her child growing up and forgetting about her.

Especially since she was probably the only parent her offspring would have.

Molly hadn't planned to wind up a single mother. Some days, she still couldn't believe she was pregnant. She hadn't told anyone about the baby yet.

Not even the father.

Guilt speared through her at the thought of Max. He deserved to know about the pregnancy, and she had every intention of telling him.

Just as soon as she figured out how.

Their relationship had been more of a fling than anything else, a series of intensely passionate encounters during his quarterly visits to The Lodge.

Molly knew he wasn't looking for anything serious, and she'd convinced herself that was fine.

Except the past few times she'd seen him, her emotions had grown stronger and stronger, demanding acknowledgment. Six months ago, she'd decided that during his next visit, she would break things off. She wanted more, but Max was totally devoted to the charity he had founded and ran.

She'd figured out what she was going to say, considered every possible reaction he might have. Then she'd steeled herself to see him again.

But he hadn't shown up.

Max had missed his regularly scheduled visit. Not a big deal, but then she'd started having symptoms, and after putting two and two together, she'd realized she was pregnant. She knew she needed to tell him, but the whole "hey, you're going to be a father" conversation was one best had in person rather than over the phone. So she was going to have to wait for his next visit to share the news.

Provided he ever came back to The Lodge. If history was any indication, he should be arriving within the next two weeks. But Molly checked the reservations regularly and his name was nowhere to be seen.

Maybe this was his way of breaking things off? If so, he was definitely not going to be happy when he heard her news. Like it or not, a baby was going to tie them together for the rest of their lives. It was a bit ironic that their casual connection had produced such a permanent bond, but life was sometimes funny that way.

The carriage shuddered a bit as someone stepped on board. Molly didn't turn around—she wanted one more moment to herself before she had to slip back into work mode.

She took a sip of water as the gondola began its journey down the mountain. Casting aside thoughts of Max, she let her gaze track across the pine trees and mountain rock, all still dusted with snow thanks to the high altitude. It was like a Christmas card come to life, a sight she didn't think she would ever grow tired of seeing.

With a small sigh, she stood. Time to greet her company on the ride down. She wasn't in her office, but she still had a duty to ensure that all guests of The Lodge were satisfied, no matter what part of the property they were using.

Molly turned, smiling as she moved. She opened her mouth to speak but as she caught sight of the other passenger, the muscles of her throat seized, trapping her words. Her eyes widened, taking in the man before her.

Tall. Broad shoulders that tapered to a slim waist. Red hair. Light green eyes. A hint of stubble, softening the lean lines of his face. And even though he was dressed for warmth, she knew that underneath his sweater and jeans he was all hard muscle and warm skin.

Heat suffused her limbs as her body responded to his presence. *Finally!* her libido seemed to say. But then her brain kicked into gear, asserting control over her raw physical reaction.

Maxwell Hollick was back.

And she was going to have to find a way to tell him she was carrying his child.

*Damn. She looks good.*

Max stared at Molly, his heart pounding hard as he drank in the sight of her. Six months between visits was way too long, but a small crisis at work had kept him occupied. Now that things were resolved, he was ready to kick back and have a little fun.

And Molly was just the woman he wanted to spend time with.

She'd changed a bit since he'd last seen her. She still had a blond bob and bright blue eyes, and her skin was as smooth and clear as he'd remembered. But she had a luminous glow about her now, and her curvaceous body seemed even more voluptuous, the swell of her hips a bit more pronounced. It was a good look for her. His fingers itched to lift the hem of her sweater and trace a line across her belly, inching higher until he could fill his hand with the soft, warm weight of her breast.

"Molly." His voice came out as a rasp, so he cleared his throat and tried again. "It's good to see you."

She blinked, her pleasant, impersonal smile slipping into a look of bewilderment as she stared at him. For a second, Max thought he saw fear flash in her eyes. But before he could wonder about it, she spoke.

"Max." Confusion and disbelief were clear in her

tone, as if she didn't quite believe he was real. "I... uh, I wasn't expecting you," she stammered.

"It was a spur-of-the-moment thing." He'd been itching to get back to The Lodge for months, to see her again. But his schedule hadn't cooperated. So he'd simply decided to force the issue—he'd had his secretary clear his schedule for a week and he'd jumped on the first plane out here. He'd arrived without a reservation, but because he was a regular guest he hadn't had any trouble scoring one of the private cabins dotting the mountaintop.

Molly nodded, but the gesture was stiff. "Well..." She trailed off, clearly searching for something to say. "I'm glad you're here."

Her expression didn't match her words, and Max had the distinct impression she was less than thrilled by his sudden appearance.

He frowned slightly, taken aback by her reaction. They hadn't parted on bad terms at the end of his last visit. Heat danced along his skin as he recalled exactly *how* they'd said goodbye. He'd left her wearing a sleepy, satisfied smile and a promise to return. So why wasn't she pleased to see him now?

Maybe she was upset because he'd been gone so long. Normally, he made it a point to stay at The Lodge every three months. But thanks to an issue with work, he'd had to skip what should have been his last visit.

"I know it's been a while," he said gruffly. "I'm sorry about that. Things got crazy at work—a big grant opportunity came up, so it was all hands on deck as we put together our application."

Max was the founder and managing director of K-9 Cadets, a charity organization that worked to provide service dogs for veterans suffering physical and psychological wounds. As a former Special Forces operative himself, Max knew all too well how the horrors of war changed a person. To make matters worse, not all casualties occurred on the battlefield—there was a depressingly large epidemic of suicide among veterans. He had decided his mission was to help his fellow veterans cope with their new normal, and in his opinion, the best way to do that was through dogs. They were the perfect companions—loyal, nonjudgmental, wonderful listeners. Not only did dogs assist with physical tasks, the emotional support they provided was sometimes the only thing standing between a veteran and the abyss.

He loved his work. More importantly, he knew how vital it was. Matching the right dog with the right vet was life-changing for everyone—quite often, it was life-*saving*, as well. That simple fact was the reason why he frequently put his personal life on hold. Therefore, as much as he enjoyed spending time with Molly here at The Lodge, he couldn't pass up the opportunity to advocate for his charity and hopefully secure more funds to expand their work.

Some of the tension left her shoulders. "Did you get the money?" Molly asked. She knew how important K-9 Cadets was to him—they'd talked about it often.

Max shrugged. "I don't know yet. It'll be a few months before we find out." He was trying not to obsess about it. He'd thought a change of scenery might help.

And hopefully Molly could distract him, as well.

He took a step forward, wanting to touch her. He'd missed her more than he cared to admit. If he had his way, he'd press her up against the one-way glass wall of the gondola so they could both enjoy the ride in a more…unorthodox way. But he didn't think she'd appreciate the idea, and he wanted to spend more than fifteen minutes getting reacquainted.

Molly didn't resist when he drew her in for a hug, but she didn't fully relax against his chest, either. She was soft and supple in his arms, but her stomach was surprisingly firm against him.

He dropped his nose to her hair, inhaling deeply. Molly's citrus and floral scent filled his lungs, triggering an avalanche of memories of their time together. It was the same movie reel he'd played in his head a thousand times over the last few months, but now it was even more vivid thanks to the woman in his arms.

"I missed you," he said softly.

"I missed you, too." Her voice was barely above a whisper, as if she was confessing something that troubled her.

He stroked her back, his fingers grazing lightly

along the valley of her spine. Gradually, she melted against him.

"I know it's been a while," he said. "But have dinner with me tonight?"

She tensed slightly. "No."

A wave of doubt washed over him. She'd never refused his invitation before. Was there someone else?

*Well, what did you expect?* he thought bitterly. *It's been six months.* It was only natural Molly had moved on. She was a beautiful woman, and he'd seen the way men looked at her.

He was so caught up in his thoughts he almost missed her next words. "I can't tonight."

"Tomorrow?" he asked, sounding a little desperate even to his own ears. *Or the next night? Or the one after?* He was only in town for a week, but if he had to wait until the end of his visit to connect with her again, he would do it without complaint.

She hesitated, then nodded against his chest. "Tomorrow is fine. I've been wanting to talk to you."

"I should have called," he said. "I meant to let you know I was going to miss my last visit. But I never got around to it."

"It's—" Her words were cut off by a deep rumble Max felt in his bones. He glanced over, expecting to see thunderclouds hovering over the town of Roaring Springs. But the sky was a clear, bright blue.

The rumble grew louder, turning into a loud roar. He shifted his gaze back to The Lodge, and the sight that greeted him turned his guts to water.

A massive wall of snow was racing down the

mountain, gaining speed as it moved. The tsunami of white rose up, seeming to dwarf the gondola as it hung precariously above the chaos below.

"Oh, my God." Molly gripped him so tightly her nails dug into his skin even through the fabric of his sweater.

The slight stinging pain snapped Max out of his shock. "It's okay," he said automatically.

"How can you say that?" Molly's voice trembled.

Because he wanted to protect her. He wanted to stand between her and the wall of snow and ice threatening to bury them.

But he was powerless against the forces of nature. And they both knew it.

They held each other, watching in silent horror as the avalanche barreled toward them. It passed underneath the carriage, seemingly with only inches to spare. Molly let out a deep breath, but Max knew they weren't out of the woods just yet.

The gondola cables were secured by a series of posts at the bottom of the mountain. If the avalanche destroyed them, well…

As though his thought had triggered it, the carriage suddenly dropped. It jerked to a hard stop, sending them both to the floor. The force of the impact wrenched Molly from his arms.

Max landed hard on his shoulder, sending a bolt of pain through the joint. There was a *thump* from somewhere to his left, and Molly let out a faint cry.

The sound sent his heart into his throat. "Molly?"

He pushed onto his knees, searching for her amid the tangle of chairs and tables strewn across the floor.

The carriage swung back and forth on its tether in a sickening lurch. "Molly?" he practically yelled her name this time.

"I'm okay," she said, though she sounded anything but. He saw movement on the other side of the carriage and began to crawl toward her.

He found her on her hands and knees, trying to stand. "Stay down," he commanded, reaching for her. He eased her into a sitting position, ignoring the protests of his shoulder every time he moved.

Molly touched her head with a grimace. When she lowered her hand, Max saw an angry red mark on her forehead. The area had already begun to swell.

"You're not okay," he said, moving to sit next to her. "Something knocked you on the head."

She grabbed his arm, her knuckles going white against the brown of his sweater. "I don't want to die here, Max."

"We won't."

Molly searched his face, her gaze pleading. "You can't say that for certain."

She was right, but he was feeling better about their chances with every second that passed. "We don't know if the main cable is down, but even if it is, the emergency cable will catch us." The backup line should be tethered to another set of poles, to maximize the chances it would still continue to function if the main line was compromised. So even if the avalanche had taken out one set of supports, hopefully the other set would remain standing. The fact that they continued to hang in the air made him think the system was working as it should.

"I hope you're right," she said.

*So do I,* he thought wryly.

The rocking motion gradually slowed and Max let out a sigh of relief. It was hard to think when the world was constantly moving. Once the carriage was still, he slowly got to his feet.

Visibility outside the gondola was bad. The air was filled with a fine powder from all the snow—it was like they were in the middle of a cloud. Gradually, though, some structures could be seen through the haze.

"The Lodge is still there," Molly said, her relief plain.

Max squeezed her hand as he looked down the mountain. "And I can see The Chateau," he added, referring to the French-inspired luxury hotel at the bottom of the mountain. "The path of the avalanche seems to have angled just enough that the place was spared." Which hopefully meant the gondola cable supports were safe, as well.

But just as he began to relax, a sharp *crack* filled the air. The carriage dropped again, only to jerk to a sudden stop once more. Molly's cry sounded like a sob, and Max reached for her as the gondola began another stomach-lurching parabola.

"It's okay. We're okay," he muttered, repeating the words in the hopes of convincing himself as much as Molly.

"Max, there's something I need to tell you."

The cables groaned under the weight of the carriage as it swung back and forth. Fear gripped Max's heart in a cold fist, and he fought the urge to panic. He took a deep breath, drawing on his Special Forces training to remain calm.

Even though there was nothing he could do.

Or was there? He glanced up, wondering if there was some way they could climb out the top of the carriage. Maybe they could hold on to the cables until rescuers arrived? *No, not likely*, he thought, dismissing the possibility as he turned his gaze down. Just how far of a drop was it? It looked like soft snow underneath—could they try to jump for it? What were the odds of a safe landing?

"Max." Molly's voice was insistent. He looked back at her, surprised to find her blue eyes full of determination.

"What is it?" His thoughts continued to whirl. How long until the rescuers would arrive? How much damage had been done by the avalanche, and would the rescuers even be able to reach them soon?

"I'm pregnant."

It took several seconds for her words to sink in. But when he finally registered what she was saying, his heart skipped a beat.

*"What?"*

She smiled nervously. "I'm pregnant," she repeated. "And it's yours."

## Chapter 2

It took at least twenty minutes for the gondola to stop its violent rocking. The carriage was never fully still—it moved a bit in response to gusts of wind, but at least the roller-coaster ride seemed to have ended.

Things appeared stable, at least for now. But Molly couldn't relax. Her heart was racing and her mouth was dry. She focused her gaze on the bottle of water she'd retrieved before the ride had even started—had it really only been half an hour since then? A mere thirty minutes ago, her life had been normal. Now she was stranded in a gondola carriage suspended high above a mountain with the father of her child her only company. Under any other circumstances, Max's presence should have been a comfort.

But thanks to her panicked confession, there was nothing but tension between them.

Not that he was talking to her. He'd been on the phone, calling everyone he knew in an attempt to get information about the search and rescue effort. He'd finally managed to connect with someone from the fire department. Molly wasn't able to hear what Blaine was saying, but if Max's reactions were anything to go by, they shouldn't be stuck here much longer.

She reached inside her purse and ran her finger along the edge of her own cell phone. She should call her parents and siblings, let them know she was okay. But she wasn't in the mood to talk to anyone, especially not in front of Max. So she typed out a quick text, reassuring her family she was fine. No one knew she was in the gondola, and that was fine by her. Later, when she was back on terra firma, she'd fill them in on all the details.

Molly slipped the phone back into her purse. Max had ended his call while she'd been texting, and she realized he was looking at her now, watching her with a hint of suspicion.

She met his gaze, lifting one eyebrow in a silent question.

"Everything okay?" he asked. His tone was heavy with meaning, but Molly didn't have the energy or the inclination to puzzle out what he was leaving unsaid.

"Yes." She considered telling him who she had contacted, then decided against it. She didn't owe him any explanations. "What did the fire department have to say?"

Max sighed and ran a hand through his hair. "The rescue effort is still getting organized. Right now, they're trying to triage the response. But they know we're up here, and we're a high priority. Hopefully, it won't take long for them to reach us."

"Maybe we'll get lucky," she murmured. Though given the way her day had gone so far, the odds were not in their favor.

They were silent for a few moments, staring out opposite windows as though they could pretend to be alone. Finally, Max cleared his throat.

"So…" he began. "You're really pregnant?"

Molly's first instinct was to fire off a sarcastic response, but she marshaled her self-control. "Yes," she said simply.

"And you're sure the baby is mine?" He winced slightly as he asked the question, as though he knew it was insensitive.

Molly narrowed her eyes. "I'm certain. Though it's good to know what you really think of me."

"I'm sorry, okay?" Max held up his hands, palms out. "But you can't blame me for asking. You're a beautiful woman, Molly. I didn't expect you to wait for me."

If she'd had any doubts about the casual nature of their relationship, his words confirmed it. He thought she had moved on. Was that because he'd done the same? The thought of him with another woman made her heart sink, but she buried the hurt. This conversation was about the baby, nothing more.

When she didn't respond, he spoke again. "How far along are you?"

"About five months."

He nodded, digesting this information. After a moment, he asked, "Why didn't you tell me?"

Anger bubbled up inside her. "I tried," she said, her voice razor-sharp. "I was going to tell you during your next visit, but you never showed up. So I called your office, wanting to know when you'd be coming back. I left several messages with your secretary, and she assured me you had received them."

Max went pale as guilt flashed across his face. "I did get them," he said quietly. "And I meant to call you back. Truly, I did. But things just got—"

"I get it," Molly said with forced lightness. "You were busy with your work, and your girlfriend and your dog." Furbert was Max's rescue dog and near-constant companion. For a brief second, her mind flashed back to the smudged print on the window of The Lodge, and in that instant she knew exactly where it had come from.

"It's not an excuse," he said. "If I had known it was urgent…" He shook his head. "Well, it doesn't matter now."

Molly noticed he hadn't refuted the comment about a girlfriend. She hugged herself and shuddered, trying not to let her imagination run wild.

"Cold?" Max asked, misinterpreting the gesture.

She shrugged. In point of fact, she *was* getting

cold. The gondola carriage had lost power, and with it, the heater. There was a definite chill in the air, which was only going to get worse as time wore on.

Max grabbed the hem of his sweater and pulled it over his head, revealing a tight-fitting cream thermal shirt underneath. Molly tried not to notice the way the waffle-weave fabric hugged his muscles, but it was a wasted effort.

He tried to hand her his sweater. "Put this on," he instructed.

Molly shot him a look. "Really? Do you think all of this—" she gestured to her breasts and stomach and hips "—is going to fit in your sweater?"

Max blushed. "I, uh… Sure."

She smiled, amused by his discomfort. "I appreciate the gesture," she said sincerely. "But I'm fine. You're better off wearing it."

Max studied her for a moment, searching her face for signs of deception. At her nod, he donned his sweater once more. The movement made him wince, though he tried to hide it.

"Are you hurt?"

He shrugged, then grunted softly. "I landed wrong on my shoulder. Nothing some ibuprofen and ice won't fix."

"Hmm." Molly wasn't convinced his assessment was correct, but she didn't bother to argue.

"We should at least sit next to each other to keep warm," he said. He settled on the floor, then reached for her hand.

It took a little effort, but Molly managed to lower

herself to the floor. She felt about as graceful as an elephant attempting ballet and briefly wondered if things were this bad now, how would she feel at nine months pregnant?

Once she was on the floor, Max scooted closer until he was sitting next to her with their sides touching. Molly hated to admit it, but she began to feel toastier right away.

"Is it a boy or a girl?" he asked softly.

"I don't know yet," she said just as quietly. "I was going to find out today. That's where I was headed— I was supposed to have a scan this afternoon."

Max took a deep breath. "I really am sorry. I should have returned your calls."

"It's fine." She waved away his apology. "You know now. That's all that matters."

He didn't reply. The temperature continued to drop in the carriage; Molly could see the fog of their breath now.

"There's no girlfriend."

He spoke so softly, Molly wasn't sure he'd said anything at all. "What?"

"There's no girlfriend," he repeated, a little louder this time. When she didn't reply, he continued. "Earlier, you said I must have been busy with work and my dog and a girlfriend. I just wanted you to know, there's no one waiting for me back home."

She turned her head away and smiled, relief warming her from the inside out. It was silly for her to care so much about his relationship status when they had never made any promises to each other. But it was nice to know she hadn't been replaced quickly.

*Hormones*, she thought, mentally shaking her head. Pregnancy had certainly done a number on her emotions.

She knew his words were an olive branch, so she responded in kind. "It's the same for me," she confided. "I haven't been with anyone else. Just you."

Max didn't reply. He lifted one arm and slowly put it around her, giving her time to reject his touch.

Molly leaned against him, partly for warmth, partly to enjoy the solid feel of him. She'd spent countless nights lying in bed, staring up at the ceiling as she remembered the time they'd spent together. Their relationship had started out as purely physical, nothing more than a fling. But somewhere along the way, she'd started to fall for the quiet ex-soldier.

And now she was pregnant with his child.

Her heart ached with the knowledge they would never be a traditional family. He lived in Washington, DC, and she lived in Roaring Springs. But even if they didn't have a geography problem, there was the small fact that he didn't love her. Still, Max was a good man, and she knew he would love his baby and do his best to be a devoted father to the little one.

And as for her? It seemed that Molly would just have to get used to being left out in the cold.

"How did this happen?" There was no blame in his voice, only curiosity.

"The usual way," she replied flatly.

She felt his eyes on her. "You know what I mean. We were always responsible."

"I know." She sighed. "But you know what they say about life and making plans…"

It was his turn to sigh. "I wasn't ready for this."

*And you think I was?* Anger flared at his words. If she didn't need his body heat, Molly would have pulled away from him then. It wasn't as though she'd planned on getting pregnant. This baby wasn't exactly part of her five-year plan, either.

But even as she silently raged against him, her anger began to fizzle. She'd had five months to process the shock from seeing those two pink lines on a stick. Max had only known he was going to be a father for thirty minutes. Maybe she could cut him a little slack.

"Me, either," she finally said. It was a hell of a thing, to find out your life was irrevocably changing. One minute, things were carrying on as normal. The next, you were a totally different person. A parent. For Molly, it had been like the flip of a switch—she wasn't pregnant, then suddenly she was. Max at least had a little time to ease into the idea of his new role before dealing with the reality of a baby.

"They'll be here soon," he said. "We'll get out of this gondola and figure out what to do."

Molly wished she shared his confidence. She wanted to believe that once they were back on the ground, everything would magically be okay. But she knew that even if the rescuers found them quickly, their issues were a long way from being resolved.

She glanced at him out of the corner of her eye. The red of his hair was evident even in the gray light streaming weakly through the glass. He was staring ahead, those soft green eyes of his unseeing as the wheels turned in his head.

He was so handsome. She'd thought so the first time she'd seen him, and time and familiarity had done nothing to erase that impression. Not for the first time, she wondered if she had been able to see into the future, would she still have gotten involved with Max? Was all this stress and worry and uncertainty worth the whirlwind fling?

As if in answer, she felt a fluttering deep inside as the baby moved. For an instant, she was filled with a sense of wonder as their unborn child kicked and stretched, exploring its world. *Yes*, she thought, as peace washed over her. She definitely hadn't planned this, and she wasn't sure what the future would hold. But now that her heart knew this little soul, she recognized that it could never be another way.

"Eight times," Max muttered next to her. He shook his head with a soft chuckle. "I just realized, we've only seen each other eight times. Feels like I've known you for longer."

"I know what you mean," Molly replied softly. They'd packed a lot of experiences into each visit. Their time together had always been intense, their connection strong. Even from the very beginning they had clicked, like two puzzle pieces fitting together.

And now they were adding a third.

It was enough to make her head throb. Of course, the fall was likely the main reason for the dull pain currently vying for her attention. The sudden motions of the gondola had tossed her around like a rag doll, and something had smacked her forehead, right along her hairline.

"How's your shoulder?" she asked, wanting a distraction.

"Eh." It wasn't much of a response, but she could tell he was uncomfortable.

"How's your head?"

"It hurts," she admitted.

Max reached for his phone. "Let me call the fire department again and see if I can get an update. You shouldn't be sitting in the cold in your condition."

Molly reached for him, grabbing his knee. He glanced at her in surprise.

"Please don't tell them I'm pregnant. No one knows."

Max's eyebrows shot up. "No one? Not even your family?"

"You're the first person I've told."

Warmth flashed in his eyes. "I suppose I should be honored."

"It's only fair." She gave him a small smile. "After all, this is your baby, too."

He pressed his lips together and nodded. Then turned his attention to his phone, tapping on the screen to dial.

Molly glanced out the window, her eyes tracking the flight of a bird as it glided by. Max began to speak, but she tuned out the sound of his voice, letting her mind wander.

*My life was simple once*, she mused. *Will it ever be that way again?*

## Chapter 3

*Two years earlier...*

"Max Hollick." Molly repeated the name to herself as she walked up the trail to the private cabin he'd rented for the week.

"We were in Special Forces together," her cousin Blaine Colton had told her earlier in the day. "He's a good buddy of mine. Good man, too. Runs a charity for vets."

"Wow," she'd said, impressed. For him to offer such praise meant Max must really be something.

"Yeah. He doesn't really take much time for himself, so this vacation is well deserved. Can you stop by and make sure he's got everything he needs to relax?"

"No problem," she'd replied. It was important to her that all guests of The Lodge were accommodated. But knowing Max was Blaine's personal friend made her want to do everything in her power to ensure he enjoyed his stay. "Is there anything in particular he likes to drink? I can drop off a bottle when he checks in."

Blaine had smiled at her. "That would be really cool of you. I know he likes brandy." He rattled off a brand, which Molly jotted into her ever-present notebook. "But he's not a huge drinker, so maybe just a small bottle?"

"I can do that," she'd promised.

Which was how she found herself standing on the doorstep of the cabin, alcohol in hand. She rapped on the door, waited for him to answer. After several minutes passed with no response, she used her master key to let herself in. She could leave the brandy on a counter with a note welcoming him to The Lodge.

Molly glanced around as she moved through the living room of the cabin. Everything looked in order, without so much as a throw pillow out of place. The back wall of the cabin was mostly windows, designed to maximize the view for the guests. The glass was spotless, the afternoon sunlight streaming through to cast the room in shades of gold. It all looked wonderful, and she made a mental note to compliment the housekeeping staff on a job well done.

The living room flowed into the kitchen, the two spaces separated by a breakfast bar. Molly set the bottle of brandy on the counter, then withdrew a card and pen from her jacket pocket and began to write a short note.

Just as she put the pen to paper, the door to the bedroom opened. She turned reflexively to see a tall man with red hair and mesmerizing green eyes standing in the doorway of the bedroom. He hadn't shaved in a few days, and the red-gold stubble on his cheeks and chin gave him a piratical air. He was handsome, the kind of man she'd take a second look at if she passed him on the street.

And he was wearing nothing but a towel around his waist.

"Whoa." He drew up short but continued to rub his hair with a towel. "Um, can I help you?"

His voice was deep and smooth, the kind that belonged on the radio. Molly swallowed hard, trying to find the words to explain her presence.

But her brain failed her. "I knocked," she blurted lamely. Against her better judgment, her eyes fixed on a droplet of water as it ran from his collarbone down his chest and over the hard, flat planes of his stomach to disappear into the cotton at his waist. He was muscled, but not overly so. It was exactly the type of body she found most attractive—fit, but not in an intimidating way.

One side of his mouth drew up in a lopsided grin. "I believe you."

A dog trotted out of the bedroom, tail held high and tongue hanging out. He looked a bit like a yellow Labrador, but his ears and nose were black, and the fur along his back was dark. He came over to her and nosed her hand in a friendly manner, then plopped down at her feet and stared up at her curiously.

"Uh…" Molly inched back, feeling decidedly out of her element.

"That's Furbert," he said, nodding at the dog. "And I'm Max. Hold on a second."

He disappeared back into the bedroom, leaving her alone with his pet. "My name is Molly Gilford," she said loudly, hoping her voice carried into the other room. "I'm the director of guest services here at The Lodge, and I was checking in to deliver a welcome gift and to make sure you have everything you need for your stay."

"Nice to meet you," he called back, sounding a little muffled. "Sorry about before. I wasn't expecting anyone."

Molly eyed Furbert, but he didn't seem worried by her presence. She began to step toward the door, needing to leave the cabin before she expired from embarrassment.

"No, that's my fault," she called out, her face growing warm. "Blaine Colton asked me to stop by. He mentioned you two were friends." And once Max related this little anecdote to Blaine, Molly was sure she'd never hear the end of it.

"Blaine's one of the best." His voice grew louder as he stepped back into the room, tugging a sweatshirt over his head. He caught sight of her as soon as the fabric cleared his face, and he lifted one eyebrow. "Leaving so soon?"

His question left her feeling even more flustered.

"Well, yes. I mean, I have to get back to work. And everything seems to be in order here." She made a show of glancing around, then nodded. "It was nice to meet you."

Max leaned against the doorjamb with his legs crossed at the ankles and his arms folded across his chest, regarding her with an amused smile as she backed toward the door. Furbert stayed where he was, but cocked his head to the side as if she were some kind of puzzle he was trying to solve.

*Almost there*, she thought as she moved. Just a few more feet, and she could escape back to her office and pretend she hadn't walked in on a nearly naked guest who just happened to be a friend of one of her cousins-turned-coworkers.

Though she had to admit, the view had been nice while it lasted.

"There is one thing you can do for me," Max called out just before she reached the door.

Molly froze, feeling a jolt of alarm. But she pasted on a smile and pretended this situation was normal. "Of course. How can I help you?" she asked politely.

"Have dinner with me."

Molly's jaw dropped open. She felt as though the bottom had disappeared from beneath her feet, leaving her hanging in midair like that cartoon coyote. Any second now, she would begin to fall.

"I…" She swallowed hard, trying to moisten her dry mouth. "I hardly think that's an appropriate question."

He pushed away from the wall and walked toward

her. *No*, she thought. *Stalked* was a better description. She stood in place, watching him as he approached. She felt like a bird, hypnotized by the green gaze of a cat as he drew near.

He stopped a few feet away. "You're right," he said. "It's not. So let me try again." He tilted his head to the side, offering her a smile that was charmingly boyish. "Will you please join me for dinner tonight?"

Molly smiled despite herself. His gaze was full of warmth, his eyes regarding her with such blatant interest it triggered a flock of butterflies in her stomach. "I can't," she said, disappointment casting a net over her nerves. Although there was no explicit company policy preventing employee-guest fraternization, she knew it was frowned upon.

He nodded in understanding. "I get it. Short notice. What about tomorrow night?"

Molly laughed at his deliberate obtuseness. "I'm the director of guest services," she said.

He nodded. "So you mentioned."

She shifted, feeling put on the spot. "You're a guest." At his blank look, she sighed. "It's not advisable…"

Max waved away the excuse. He leaned forward, lowering his voice to a conspiratorial whisper. "What's life without a little risk?"

He had a point. And it had been a long time since she'd been on a date. The Lodge was booked year-round, making it difficult for Molly to carve time out of her schedule for a personal life. Since she hadn't met a man she wanted to get to know better, it was all too easy for her to focus on work.

"Don't think of it as a date," he advised.

"Then how should I think of it?" She was enjoying this flirty back-and-forth, maybe a little too much.

"A work function."

"Ah, but I don't usually have dinner with guests as part of my job."

This logical statement did nothing to deter him. "So you're saying I'm the first?"

She laughed. "I haven't agreed yet."

Amusement flashed in his green eyes. "Yet. That means you will."

Molly's resistance was fading in the face of his interest. In truth, she would like to have dinner with him. She just wasn't sure it was a good idea.

"I'll be a gentleman," he promised, holding his hands up as if to demonstrate his innocence. "No funny business."

*Damn*, she thought, shocking herself. It really had been too long since she'd received any male attention if she was disappointed by his promise of good behavior. *I've got to get a life*.

She bit her bottom lip. His gaze zeroed in on the gesture, heat flashing in his eyes.

*Why wait?*

"All right," she said, deciding to throw caution to the wind. "Where would you like to meet? And what time?"

He smiled. "How does seven sound? And we can stay right here. That way you don't have to worry about anyone seeing you with me outside of working hours."

He was teasing her, but she did appreciate his discretion. Roaring Springs might be a tourist destination, but it was a small town at heart. Molly knew that as a grown adult, she had a right to a social life. But she also knew the town regulars, and her extended family, would waste no time commenting on her choices. She simply didn't have the patience to deal with the gossip right now.

"Seven works for me," she said. "What can I bring?"

Max tilted his head to the side. "A bottle of wine? If you're comfortable with that."

Molly nodded. "Red or white?"

He considered the question for a moment. "Red, I think."

"Are you actually going to cook?" The thought made her smile. Max looked like the kind of man who could run a grill, but she had a hard time picturing him in the kitchen.

He threw his shoulders back and puffed out his chest. "Do you doubt my abilities?" He sounded serious, but there was a twinkle in his eyes. Furbert woofed softly, as if to vouch for his master's culinary skills.

Molly shook her head. "I would never question your talents," she said with mock seriousness. "I'm sure whatever you prepare will be wonderful."

Max nodded solemnly. "I'm glad one of us thinks so." He winked at her, then stepped in close.

Molly gasped at his sudden nearness. For a split second, she thought he was going in for a kiss. Then he reached past her, his hand landing on the doorknob.

He opened the door in one fluid motion. "I'll see you tonight," he said simply.

Molly nodded, relief and disappointment flooding her system in equal measure. "Later," she replied softly. She took a deep breath, inhaling detergent, soap and warm male skin as she moved past him.

She set off down the path, feeling his eyes on her as she walked.

But she didn't look back.

*Four hours later...*

Max dumped the last of the food from the take-out containers into serving dishes, then stuck them into the oven to keep warm. Furbert watched him as he wadded up the trash, stuffing it down into the can.

"What?" he asked the dog. "I can't serve her out of the foil trays. That would be tacky."

Furbert cocked his head to the side and barked in reply. It sounded accusatory to Max's ears.

"No, I'm not going to tell her I cooked," he said defensively. "But it's not my fault if she assumes I did."

The dog barked again, clearly unimpressed.

"Oh, whatever," Max muttered. "You wouldn't understand."

Furbert jumped onto the couch and flopped down on the cushions with a sigh.

"We talked about this," Max said. "Get down."

Furbert flicked his tail once in acknowledgment of Max's words, then closed his eyes.

"Brat." But there was no heat in his voice. Max couldn't bring himself to chastise the dog. Furbert was his constant companion, his best friend since he'd returned home from his last tour of duty.

Max had loved his life as a Green Beret. The men he'd worked with had been the best in the business, their training second to none. Every single one of them had been smart, professional and passionate about their work.

But Special Forces wasn't just a job. It was a calling, an all-consuming lifestyle that required commitment and discipline. In return, the team had been his family. Max wouldn't have hesitated to lay down his life to save any one of his brothers-in-arms, and he knew the feeling was mutual. The bonds forged among them all were unbreakable and thicker than any blood connection.

Or marriage vows.

Most of the guys weren't married. The few old-timers who were had managed to snag women who were former military brats. They knew the life, understood the sacrifices. There had been a few divorces during his tenure as an operative, but some of the guys actually made the whole marriage and family thing work.

Max had thought he was one of them. His wife,

Beth, had seemed happy. In the beginning, she'd been determined to be the perfect military wife. She'd joined several social organizations for spouses, written him regularly when he was on tour and welcomed him home with gusto when he returned.

But at some point, things started to change. Max couldn't quite put his finger on when things shifted between them, but gradually the stream of letters slowed to a trickle, and her welcome-home smile started to look a little strained.

Then the fights started. Arguments over stupid stuff, like not loading the dishwasher correctly. Beth nitpicked everything he touched, to the point Max felt like he couldn't do anything right. And while part of him understood the spats were really a symptom of larger issues, the rest of him was simply relieved to go overseas again. He'd take people shooting at him over an unhappy wife any day.

He'd done a lot of thinking during that last tour. About the state of his life and where he wanted to end up twenty years from then. Being an operative was incredibly fulfilling, but it was a young man's game. One day he'd wake up and discover he was too old to keep up with the physical demands of the job. His knees already ached in the morning, and he'd twisted his ankle more times than he could count. At some point, his physical limitations were going to be a liability to the team.

And what then? He wasn't the type to sit behind a desk for the rest of his working life. Nor did he want to join the ranks of the military brass. Max knew he wanted to stay connected to the military, but he didn't want to continue to wear the uniform.

The issue dogged his thoughts for the first several weeks of his tour. Until one day, the solution came trotting up on four legs.

His team had been on patrol—standard stuff, nothing unusual. But when they'd stopped for a break, they'd been joined by a scrawny yellow puppy with big black eyes and an inquisitive personality.

"Hey there, buddy," he'd said as the dog nosed his leg. "What are you doing out here?"

"Probably searching for food," one of his teammates said. "Look at how skinny he is."

"Poor guy," said another.

Taking pity on the friendly puppy, the men had dug through their pockets and come up with offerings of beef jerky and a peanut butter granola bar. Max wasn't sure if it was safe for dogs to eat peanut butter, but the stray scarfed it down before he could finish asking the question.

Max had offered him some water, and after his snack, the dog curled up at his feet and fell asleep with a contented sigh.

"He's really sweet," Max remarked.

"Yeah," his buddy Joseph said. "But don't go getting any ideas. You know you can't bring him back to base."

Max nodded in acknowledgment. The team rose to get back to it, and Max felt a pang in his heart as he looked at the sleeping dog. He was in for a rough life. *Just like everybody else in this desert.* He knew he couldn't save everyone, but there was something especially frustrating about the fact that he couldn't help a dog who had such simple needs compared with his human neighbors.

"Shake it off, Hollick," Brad, the team leader, said. "You can't fit a dog in your duffel anyway."

"Yeah, I know," Max replied, turning his thoughts to the mission at hand.

But damned if he didn't look behind him an hour later to find the dog trotting after them, tail wagging despite the desert heat.

"Your friend is back," Joseph observed. They were headed to base now, having wrapped up their patrol for the day.

"Looks like," Max concurred. He tried to quash the spurt of excitement bubbling up in his chest. Even though the puppy had followed the team, there was no home for him on the base.

The group stopped again for a short break, giving the dog time to catch up. "Somebody's got a crush on you, Max," Joseph teased.

"Ha ha," Max said. He wandered a few feet away, searching for a modicum of privacy so he could relieve his bladder. But as he stepped off the path, the dog barked. He turned around to find the animal staring intently at him, as if he was trying to tell him something.

"Stay there," he told the dog. "I'll be right back."

He turned around only to hear another bark, but he ignored this one. He took two steps when Joseph let out a surprised yelp. A blast of yellow zoomed past him, and Max suddenly found himself faced with a snarling bundle of yellow fur and bones.

"Easy, boy," he said, taking a step back. What was going on with this dog? One minute, he was friendly and sweet and the next he was acting possessed. Maybe it wasn't such a bad thing that he was going to have to stay in the desert…

Brad and Joseph and some of the other men came up behind him. The puppy increased his snarling, punctuating it with loud barks for added effect.

"What's the deal?" Brad asked. "Do we need to put him down?"

Max watched the dog carefully. If someone took a step forward, he became more aggressive, going so far as to lunge forward with a snap. But when the men took a step back, he relaxed.

He heard the creak of a strap as someone shifted their rifle. "No," he said, holding up his hand. "I think he's trying to tell us something."

Max glanced at the ground behind the dog. It was strewn with rocks and a few pieces of fabric and paper, faded from their time spent baking in the sun. Nothing looked unusual or out of place.

Except…there was one pile of rocks that looked a little *too* neat. Max pulled out his binoculars and trained them on the spot. As he focused on the ground, his blood ran cold.

There was definitely something under those rocks. He couldn't make out all the details, but he did see the curve of a wire protruding from the pile.

"There's an IED out there," he reported grimly, lowering the binoculars.

"Where?" Brad's voice was intense, urgent. A frisson of energy crackled through the rest of the men. They began to study the ground with new interest, searching for additional threats.

Max pointed out the device to the men. "I'll be damned," Brad muttered. "Let's call it in."

They were still a few miles away from base, but this was a popular trail used for foot patrols. The area was routinely swept for explosives. Either this one had been missed, or it was a recent plant.

The radio dispatcher called up the explosive ordnance team, which sent out a group right away.

"Back on the trail," Brad ordered. "No one goes off, not even to take a piss."

The men retreated to the relative safety of the marked path. As they moved away, the puppy visibly relaxed. Once everyone was on the trail again, he morphed back into the friendly animal they had encountered before—tail up, tongue lolling out, a big doggy smile on his face.

He walked over to Max and licked his hand, then sat in the dirt and stared up at him with his head cocked to the side. Max knew dogs couldn't talk, but he swore the pup was giving him an "Are we cool?" look.

"Oh, yeah." Max knelt in the dirt next to the dog, pulling him close for a hug. "You saved our lives." He tried to ignore the way his stomach twisted as his body caught up to the realization that he'd narrowly missed being blown to bits.

The rest of the team wandered over as they waited for the ordnance guys. Everyone had a pat and a kind word for the animal. Even Brad softened toward the dog.

"Looks like we have a new member of the team," he remarked.

"Really?" Max couldn't keep the hope out of his voice. There was no way he was going to leave this dog in the desert now, but if the rest of his team was on board, it would be a lot easier to sneak him on base and take care of him.

Brad knelt to pat the dog. He slid a glance at Max, then returned his eyes to the dog. "Sometimes it's better to ask for forgiveness than permission," he said, appearing to talk to no one at all.

Max turned his head so the other man wouldn't see his smile. "Understood, sir," he said.

And that was that. The team had helped him bring the dog on base, christening him Furbert. It wasn't Max's first choice for a name, but one of the guys on the team said it was an old French term having to do with armor. "He protected us," his friend had said. "We have to give him his due."

From that point on, Furbert became the unofficial mascot of the team. The other people on base turned a blind eye to the sight of the dog loping next to Max, and for his part, he made sure Furbert was cared for and well-fed. He even convinced one of the doctors on base to examine his friend to make sure he was healthy. After a few doses of deworming medication, Furbert began to put on weight until he no longer resembled a skeleton with fur, but rather a happy, spoiled young dog.

Max would have loved Furbert regardless, but it was his actions one afternoon that sealed his place in the hearts of everyone on base.

Medevac arrived with a chopper full of injured men. The medical team began working on them right away. About an hour later, the rest of the patrol staggered into base. By this time, a small crowd had developed outside the field hospital as people milled about waiting for news. Max was there, along with his fellow operatives. Furbert sat at his feet, as usual.

A few men pushed through the crowd to the front, intent on going inside. A third man trailed after them, catching them before they could enter the hospital. "Stay here," he said. His insignia showed him to be the officer in charge of the unit. "I'll go check for an update."

The two men stopped, though it was clear they didn't like it. They were kitted out for patrol, their faces grimy with sweat and dust. Both of them sported dull red patches on their knees.

*Blood*, Max thought grimly. It was the telltale stain of someone who had knelt by an injured colleague in a desperate battle to help them.

The officer went inside, leaving the two men oblivious to the crowd surrounding them. Max could tell by the looks on their faces they were focused on their friends inside the hospital, silently bargaining with the universe for the survival of their injured comrades.

After several minutes of silence, the officer returned. One look at his face, and everyone knew.

"Baker?" one of the men choked out.

The officer nodded. "And Jeffries."

One man sank to the ground while the other stood frozen in place, unwilling or unable to believe the bad news.

The officer began to comfort his men. Max and the rest of the crowd stirred, knowing it was time to leave. This was a private moment, one that didn't warrant public scrutiny.

He motioned for Furbert to follow, but the dog refused to budge. "Come on, boy," he said sternly. "Let's go."

To his horror, the dog walked over to the grieving soldiers. He nudged the man who was on his knees, as if to say, "I'm here."

Max took a step forward with the intent of retrieving the animal. But the soldier didn't seem to mind. In fact, he appeared to welcome the dog's presence. Without saying a word, he opened his arms and embraced Furbert, dropping his head against the young dog's side.

For his part, Furbert was content to sit still and let the soldier's tears soak into his fur. Max watched the pair of them from several feet away, marveling at the way the dog's mere presence brought obvious comfort to a man who was having one of the worst days of his life. *This is it*, he realized with dawning wonder. *This is what I can do.*

He was going to retire after this tour and devote his time to pairing dogs with veterans. If anyone could use comfort, it was the men and women who had seen the horrors of war. And there was nothing like the nonjudgmental presence of a dog to make it seem like things were going to be okay.

It was perfect. And best of all, Beth would be glad to have him home again.

It had taken months and a virtual forest's worth of paperwork. But Furbert had eventually made it back to the States. Max had never been so happy to see anyone before in his life.

Beth, on the other hand, had been less than impressed.

She'd initially been excited after he retired from the service. She'd even expressed support for his idea of starting a charity—K-9 Cadets, he'd decided to call it. But as he'd settled in to start the work, she'd grown more and more distant.

One night, he confronted her. "I thought you wanted this," he said. He gestured to himself as they stood in the kitchen. "You used to beg me to retire, to get out of Special Forces and find a normal job."

"I know." Her voice was dull, as though she couldn't muster the energy for this discussion.

"So what's changed? Why do you seem so unhappy now that I'm home?"

She turned to hang up the dish towel, shoulders heaving with a sigh. "I can't do this anymore."

A chill skittered down Max's spine. "What are you saying?"

Beth whirled to face him, her expression thunderous. "I'm saying I'm done! I want out of this marriage!"

Max stared at her, emotions swirling in his chest. His first reaction was disbelief—surely she wasn't serious? Except he could tell by the look in her eyes she wasn't joking.

Anger burned away his confusion. What the hell was wrong with her? He'd turned his life upside down to please her, retiring earlier than he had originally planned all so they could spend more time together and work on their marriage. And now, after he'd made so many sacrifices, she'd decided his efforts weren't good enough?

He looked at her, studying her face as though he'd never seen her before. There had been a time when he'd known her every expression, could even predict her thoughts. Now she was a stranger. Max searched for any signs of the woman he'd fallen in love with, but she wasn't there.

Perhaps she hadn't been there for a while.

"Don't try to tell me you're happy," she said. Her voice was softer now, almost pleading.

"I'm not," he admitted. "But I wasn't ready to give up on our marriage."

She glanced away. "You were never here."

"I'm here now." He thought about reaching for her, decided against it. Some part of him sensed there would be no reconciliation, though hope still glimmered at the edges of his thoughts.

"Not really. You're so wrapped up in your charity and that damn dog."

He couldn't deny it. But that didn't mean he was going to accept all the blame.

"This isn't only my fault, Beth. Yes, I was gone a lot. But you knew what you were signing up for when you married me. And even when I was home between tours, you didn't seem to want to reconnect."

"You weren't the same person I married," she shot back.

"I could say the same about you," he said.

Beth sighed, shook her head. "Why are we arguing about this? Neither one of us is happy. Let's just call it a wash and walk away."

She had a point. Why prolong the inevitable? If she wanted to leave, he wasn't going to stop her. Max had his pride—he wouldn't beg her to stay.

Her phone buzzed on the counter. She glanced at it, and in that instant, Max saw longing in her eyes.

Suddenly, he knew.

"Who is he?" His voice was cold. He waited for the jolt of surprise, but it never came. Deep down, he'd known this day was coming.

Her cheeks flushed, and she shot him a guilty look. "No one you know."

Max merely nodded. Then he turned and walked out of the room.

*Lesson learned*, he thought bitterly as he packed his things. He'd left the house and never looked back.

It had been three years since that conversation in the kitchen. Now he stood in a different kitchen, with anticipation instead of dread thrumming through his veins.

He wasn't sure what had made him ask Molly to join him for dinner. He certainly wasn't looking for a relationship—his charity work took up all his time, and he was okay with that.

But there was something about her that called to him. It wasn't just her appearance, though there was no denying she was attractive. Blond hair that looked like spun gold, big blue eyes, voluptuous curves in all the right places; Molly Gilford was an incredibly beautiful woman. Beyond that, though, there was a sweetness in her eyes, a lightness of spirit that called to him.

She hadn't played coy when he'd walked out half-naked, hadn't tried to flirt with him. No, she'd been genuinely embarrassed.

It was a refreshing, unexpected reaction. It made him want to spend more time with her.

And unless he missed his guess, she wanted to see him, too.

Her initial refusal had seemed like a knee-jerk reaction, something she'd said because she thought she had to. Even as the words had left her mouth, he could tell by the look on her face she was considering the possibility. It was her mixed signals that had made him ask again. He wasn't a fan of harassing women, and he definitely knew how to take no for an answer. But Molly's response had been conflicted enough to warrant another try.

He was glad she had decided to give him a chance.

"We need to be on our best behavior tonight," he said to Furbert. "Don't jump on her when she walks through the door."

Furbert's tail thumped against the cushion, though he didn't bother to open his eyes.

"Right," Max muttered to himself. "Same goes for me."

Tonight was just about dinner. But hopefully the next time could be about something more…

# Chapter 4

Molly stood on the welcome mat of Max's cabin for the second time that day, holding another bottle of alcohol.

"It's not a real date," she muttered. In the hours since she'd accepted his dinner invitation, Molly had tried to convince herself she was merely fulfilling her responsibilities as director of guest services. This was a chance for her to do a more thorough inspection of the private cabins, to ensure they were equipped to meet every guest's needs. Furthermore, she had promised Blaine she would make sure Max was well taken care of. Tonight's dinner was an opportunity to get a better idea of what he would need to make his stay as restful and enjoyable as possible.

"This is business. Nothing personal."

But it certainly *felt* personal.

She knocked on the cabin door, anticipation fluttering like butterflies in her stomach as she waited for Max to answer. Their first meeting had been… memorable, to say the least. Part of her still felt a little embarrassed about catching him fresh from the shower. But that hadn't stopped her from reliving the experience all afternoon. The sight of him all shirtless and damp and warm had been running through her mind on an endless loop.

If she'd been more daring, she would have touched him. Just reached out and trailed her finger along the water droplets running down his torso. He would have sucked in a breath, and her touch would have given him goose bumps. She would have smiled at him, one of those smiles that says more than words ever could. He would have smiled back, then pulled her in close for a hot kiss…

Her fantasy was interrupted by the man himself opening the door. Molly jumped but tried to cover it with a smile.

"Welcome back." Max grinned at her and pulled the door wide so she could step inside.

Her cheeks warmed as she moved past him. Did he have any idea she'd just been daydreaming about him? Hopefully her thoughts weren't that transparent.

He reached for the bottle of wine, his hand brushing hers as he took it from her. "Thanks for this," he said, not even bothering to glance at the label before setting it on a nearby table. Then he moved back, his hands on her shoulders as he helped her shrug out of her coat. He never touched her skin, but a shiver ran through her nonetheless.

*Get it together*, she told herself. *He hasn't really touched you.*

*Not yet, anyway*, said a traitorous voice in her head.

She turned back to Max, thanking him for taking her coat.

"My pleasure," he said. He picked up the bottle of wine and gestured for her to move forward. "I'll get this opened so it can breathe."

Molly followed him a few steps but paused when she caught sight of the dog on the couch. "He looks comfortable."

The dog cocked an ear, his eyes still closed. Apparently deciding she wasn't worth the effort, he relaxed again with a soft doggy sigh.

Max glanced back, holding the wine bottle and opener. He looked at the dog, an indulgent smile on his face. "I can't tell you how many times I've told him to stay off the furniture."

"So you're saying he's a good listener."

Max laughed. The sound was deep and joyful and it rolled into her chest and warmed her from the inside out. He returned to the kitchen and she followed, suddenly wanting to give him a reason to laugh again.

It smelled wonderful, the aromas of something hot and Italian heavy in the air. Her stomach growled loudly; she pressed a hand over it and glanced up to see if Max had noticed.

He had.

"I'm hungry, too," he said with a smile. "Let's talk while we eat."

Molly offered to help, but Max shooed her away. "You're my guest," he said.

She appreciated his manners, especially as it gave her an opportunity to watch him move around the kitchen. He wore jeans and a dark green button-down shirt that enhanced his eyes. The sleeves were rolled up, a casual look that she found sexy. His forearms were dusted with fine red-gold hairs; the lamplight in the dining area made his skin look gilded.

In a matter of minutes, he had the table set and the food in place. He poured her a glass of wine, gesturing for her to sit across from him.

Molly hid a smile as he plated the food. The lasagna looked amazing, and also quite familiar. Che Bello was the best Italian place in Roaring Springs— apparently, it hadn't taken Max long to find it.

But would he take credit for the food? Molly decided to test him, curious to see how he would react. Would he tell her the truth? Or would he pretend to have cooked everything himself, soaking up praise for a job he hadn't done?

Either way, his reaction would tell her something about who he was as a man.

*Let's see if you're as good a guy as Blaine says*, she thought wryly.

"This is delicious," she remarked, careful to keep any hint of suspicion out of her voice.

He smiled. "I'm glad you like it."

"Where did you learn to cook like this?"

Max took a sip of wine. "Oh, it's just something I picked up along the way."

Molly considered his response as she took another bite. Technically, he *was* telling the truth. She decided to push a little harder.

"Let me guess—you have an Italian grandmother who taught you everything she knows?"

"Ah, not exactly." He shifted a bit in his seat, the tips of his ears turning pink.

His embarrassment made her feel a little better about their encounter this afternoon. He'd been so cool and collected the whole time, as if it was no big deal she'd walked in on him in a towel. It was kind of nice to have the shoe on the other foot.

"You know," she said, deciding to put him out of his misery, "there's a place in town that makes lasagna almost as good as yours. It's called Che Bello. Maybe you saw it on the drive in?"

Max choked a bit on his wine, his eyes flying up to meet her gaze. He dabbed at his mouth with a napkin, a sheepish smile forming on his lips.

"You got me," he said. "But in my defense, I never said I actually made it."

Molly laughed softly. "No, you didn't."

He studied her from across the table, his eyes bright with curiosity. "You're not like most women, are you?"

The question surprised her, and she took a sip of wine to stall. "I'm not sure," she finally said. "In what way?"

He lifted one shoulder in a shrug. "A lot of the women I know wouldn't have teased me about the food. And they definitely wouldn't have been bothered by catching me just out of the shower."

"Oh, no?"

He shook his head. "Most of them would have seen it as an invitation."

She tsked at him. "You poor thing. I'm sure you have to beat the ladies off with a stick." It was a scenario she didn't care to imagine, and frankly she found this line of conversation tiring. If Max was going to spend the evening emphasizing his conquests, she was going to fake a headache and leave soon. She didn't get a lot of time off, and she wasn't interested in spending it with a man who wanted to talk about his various friends-with-benefits arrangements.

He laughed, another full-throated rumble that wrapped around her like a blanket. "Oh, hardly," he said. "I haven't dated anyone in over a year. But I spend a lot of time trying to raise money for my foundation, and I meet a lot of unhappily married women." He shook his head. "Some of them have offered large donations in exchange for a bit of adventure."

Molly's annoyance faded in the face of his candid explanation. "That must make things awkward."

It had to be difficult, trying to let the wives down easy so their husbands would donate to his charity.

"Yeah. It's a tough needle to thread sometimes." He took another bite of lasagna, then nodded at her. "But enough about me. I want to know more about you."

"There's not much to tell," she said, scooping more food onto her fork. Molly had never felt comfortable talking about herself, a fact that wasn't about to change now. Still, she appreciated his interest and wanted to keep the conversation flowing. "I grew up in the area, started working at The Lodge during my summer breaks as a teenager. I went to college in Denver, then came back here."

"How long have you known Blaine?"

"Oh, for a while," she said with a smile. "Seeing as how he's my cousin."

"Ah, so you joined the family business."

She shrugged. "In a manner of speaking, yes."

Max took another sip of wine. "Well, for what it's worth, between you and Blaine it's clear you got the looks."

It was an obvious attempt at flattery, but it made Molly's stomach flutter nonetheless. "Better not tell him," she said. "You'll break his heart."

Max shot her a conspiratorial grin. "That's a risk I'm willing to take."

Molly took another drink, surprised to see the bottom of her glass. She had a pleasant buzz going, despite the fact that Max hadn't poured her a large glass.

He reached for the bottle, brows lifted in question. Molly shook her head. "Not right now."

"Already feeling the effects?" he teased.

She nodded. "What can I say? I'm a cheap date."

"I'll keep that in mind for the next time," he murmured.

Molly felt her face flush. "Tell me about your charity." Blaine had mentioned it once or twice, but she was curious to know more.

Max dabbed at his mouth with a napkin. "It's called K-9 Cadets. Basically, we work to pair military veterans with service dogs."

"Oh, wow." That sounded impressive. "How does that work?"

"It starts when a veteran contacts us. We meet with them to determine what kind of support they need, then we begin the process of matching them with a dog."

"How do you find the dogs? I don't imagine you can pick them up at the local shelter."

"You'd be surprised," Max commented. "We do scan the shelters regularly to identify animals that look promising. If we find one, we'll adopt the dog and start training."

It sounded fascinating, and so far removed from Molly's daily activities. "You train the dogs, too?"

He shook his head. "We partner with several organizations who go through the nuts and bolts of training. But we're involved with it, and we look at how the animal behaves during training to help pair them with a veteran."

"What do the dogs do?" Molly's experience with canines was limited to her friends' pets. She was more of a cat person, though she liked dogs as a rule.

"That depends," Max said. "For veterans who have physical limitations, we pair them with a dog who has been trained to assist in daily tasks. Other veterans need emotional support, so in those cases, we pair them with an animal whose training reflects that."

Molly reached for the wine bottle, fascinated. "Was Furbert your first match?"

"In a manner of speaking." He told her how the dog had found him during a patrol in the desert. Molly glanced at the couch while he spoke. It was hard to imagine the happy, healthy-looking dog as a bony puppy. But she recalled the intelligence in his eyes when he'd met her a few hours ago, and could easily picture him warning Max and his men about the bomb.

Tears pricked her eyes as he described the way Furbert had comforted the mourning soldiers.

"That's when I knew," Max said. "Every veteran deserves that kind of support. So I made it my mission to help them."

Molly sniffed. "That's very noble."

"I don't know about that." He passed her a napkin, and she swiped her eyes dry. "Don't go thinking I'm a hero," he said. "I came back whole. Not everyone does."

"True, but you were willing to sacrifice yourself.

Not everyone signs up for that risk. That's pretty heroic if you ask me."

Max looked down, took a sip of his wine. It was clear he wasn't comfortable with her praise. But Molly knew it was the truth.

Something cold nudged her elbow. She looked down to find Furbert sitting by her chair, staring up at her.

She smiled down at him. "I'm okay, buddy." She glanced at Max, saw him watching them with a smile. "Can I pet him?"

"Sure, but just know that once you do, you've made a friend for life."

She stroked his head, tentatively at first, then with gradually increasing pressure. Furbert's fur was soft, his ears like warm velvet. He sighed with pleasure and rested his head in her lap as she ran her hand along his head and down his back. There was something deeply soothing about petting a dog, especially one who apparently enjoyed it so much. The stress of her day melted away as she scratched Furbert's ears, and for the first time, she understood why her friends thought their dogs were worth the effort it took to take care of them.

"Would you like to move to the den?"

"That sounds nice." Molly picked up her glass and followed Max to the sofa with Furbert trotting at her heels.

Max sat on one end of the couch and she sat on the other. Furbert took the middle cushion, resting his head in Molly's lap and wagging his tail in Max's. "He's so sweet," she said.

"He really is," Max agreed. "He's very sensitive to moods, and if he thinks someone is upset, he doesn't hesitate to try to comfort them."

"I'm glad you found him." It broke her heart to think of him wandering alone out in the desert, trying to survive under the unforgiving sun.

"I think it was the other way around," Max said with a smile. "But I agree with your sentiment."

They fell into an easy conversation, talking about everything and nothing. Max was so easy to talk to, Molly found herself confessing her irrational fear of birds. She bit her lip, expecting him to laugh at her the way most people did. But he merely looked at her with kind eyes.

"That must be hard," he said. "Especially living here, with all the wildlife."

"It's rough sometimes," she admitted. "I'm not paralyzed by fear to the point I can't go outside. But there are definitely some tough moments."

"I'm afraid of spiders," he said.

Molly eyed him, trying to decide if he was being serious or just hoping to make her feel better.

Apparently, her expression gave away her thoughts. "It's true," he insisted. "I hate them."

"They're not my favorite, either," she said.

"Too many eyes, too many legs." He shuddered. "They creep me out. The small ones I can handle, but you should have seen some of the spiders that live in the desert."

Molly wrinkled her nose. "No, thank you."

He laughed. "There was one time we were out on patrol, and we stopped for a short break. I sat on a big rock and started dumping the sand out of my boots. My buddies started laughing, but they wouldn't tell me why. My friend Joseph waited until I had my boots back on, then pointed behind me. I turned around and found a camel spider sitting in my shadow." He shook his head at the memory. "I jumped straight up into the air with a scream that nearly ruptured my team's eardrums."

"Oh, man." Molly laughed. "If I had a bird that close to me, I'd die of a heart attack."

"I nearly did," he said. "Logically, I know they're not dangerous to humans. He was just trying to get some relief from the sun. But in the moment, all I could think about was getting far, far away."

"Was Furbert with you then?"

"I'd left him on base. And I'm not ashamed to admit I gave him a big hug when I got back."

The dog's tail thumped against the cushion, as if he knew they were talking about him.

"It's a good thing you had him," Molly said, stroking his fur.

"No kidding," Max replied. "Especially since I wasn't getting any sympathy from the rest of the guys on my team."

Molly laughed and glanced out the window. Night had fallen while they'd talked, turning the pine trees from green to black. Soft lights illuminated the path from the cabin's back door to a hiking trail, and in their yellow glow, she saw fat snowflakes dropping silently to the ground. It would be cold outside, a marked contrast to the cozy warmth of the cabin.

She glanced back to the sofa. Furbert's head was a welcome weight in her lap. The wine, the food and the dog had left her feeling content in a way she hadn't experienced in a long time. The evening had evolved in an unexpected direction, thanks mostly to the man sitting nearby.

Molly had found Max attractive from the start, but he was even more appealing to her now. She hadn't thought they would be so compatible; in truth, she had expected him to be focused so completely on his job he wouldn't want to talk about much else.

Nothing had been further from the truth.

*This is what dating is supposed to feel like*, she told herself. It had been so long since she'd made an effort to connect with a man, she'd almost forgotten how nice it could be.

Too bad she'd rediscovered this feeling with a guest who would be leaving soon.

Molly met his eyes. She needed to leave now, before she got too comfortable here. This had been a pleasant evening, but it was not going to lead to anything more. Max and his dog would return to their normal lives, and she would remain here.

"You're going to leave, aren't you?"

Molly blinked at his question, which eerily echoed her own thoughts. Max sounded equal parts disappointed and understanding, matching her mood perfectly.

"It is getting late," she said. Reluctantly, she shifted on the seat, disturbing Furbert. He lifted his head, clearly confused as to why she would choose to interrupt their comfortable arrangement. "Sorry, buddy," she said to him.

The dog emitted a long-suffering sigh and jumped to the floor. Max stood, holding out his hand. Molly slid her hand into his, palm against palm.

She stood, the sudden change in position making her head spin. Or maybe that was her proximity to Max? He hadn't stepped back to give her room, so now only inches separated them.

He smelled even better than she remembered. This close, she could see the flutter of his pulse in his neck. She leaned forward a bit, smiling to herself as she watched the beat speed up in response to her movement.

She lifted her gaze to meet his eyes. "Thank you for dinner," she said softly. "I had a nice time."

"So did I," he replied. His voice was quiet, hardly more than a low rumble that made her think of thunder from a distant storm.

Molly knew she should turn around and walk out the door. But her feet felt rooted in place, unable or perhaps unwilling to move.

"Let me get your coat," Max offered. Except he didn't move, either. They stood there next to the couch, locked in each other's gravitational pull. Who would be the first to break away?

The air between them crackled with awareness. Alcohol and anticipation were a potent combination in Molly's system, making her feel simultaneously languid and hyperalert to any subtle changes in Max's body.

Slowly, cautiously, he dipped his head. Molly recognized the invitation, and rose up on her toes. They met in the middle, lips brushing hesitantly before fully committing to the kiss.

Max's mouth was hot and tasted of wine. Molly placed her hands on his shoulders, needing to anchor herself in place so she could fully embrace the sensations running through her. Sparks of desire zinged through her limbs and settled into her core, making her feel as though she were holding a live wire.

He trailed the tip of his tongue along her bottom lip. Molly opened her mouth with a moan, her body practically melting against his. He was warm and solid and he wrapped his arms around her, filling her senses with his taste, his scent, his touch.

She tightened her grip on Max's shoulders, her fingers digging into the fabric of his shirt. It wasn't enough. She needed more—more contact, more access. More of him.

Molly slid her hands down the flat expanse of his chest. She knew from their initial meeting he was leanly muscled, and she felt the solid strength of him under her fingertips. But before she could settle into an exploration of his body, he distracted her by skimming one hand down the side of her torso. Goose bumps sprang up in the wake of his touch, despite the fact that he hadn't actually made contact with her skin.

His hand rose up again, brushing the side of her breast. Her breath caught in her throat as he fit his palm around her curve. She stilled, deliciously shocked by the sensation of a man's hands on her body.

But Max immediately dropped his arm and pulled away, breaking the kiss. "I'm sorry," he said, touching his mouth with the back of his hand. "I shouldn't have done that."

Molly shook her head, her mind still trying to process what was transpiring between them. "I'm fine. It's fine," she stammered.

"I didn't mean to make you uncomfortable," he said, as if he hadn't heard her. "My brain just went out the window when we started kissing."

She laughed softly, happy to hear she wasn't the only one who'd been so affected. "I know the feeling."

Max ran a hand though his hair and smiled down at her. She saw a mix of emotions in his eyes: arousal, relief and amusement. His apparent feelings mirrored her own, which was another point in his favor.

But now that she was no longer distracted by the feel of his mouth on hers, Molly started to remember all the reasons why her attraction to him was a bad idea. Whatever this was between them couldn't go anywhere. And while it might be fun to try a no-strings-attached fling, was her heart really capable of staying on the sidelines?

It was a big risk, one Molly wasn't sure she should take.

"Let me get your coat," Max said gruffly.

He stepped away, leaving her with an odd sense of disappointment. Truly, she'd never felt such immediate chemistry with anyone before. A small part of Molly acknowledged that if he hadn't misinterpreted her reaction, they would probably be in bed right now.

*It's better this way*, she told herself as Max helped her don her coat and they parted ways.

But as she trudged along the snow-dusted trail to the main building, she couldn't help but wonder if that was the truth.

It was a beautiful day. So why wasn't he enjoying it more?

Max reached the bottom of the ski run and moved to the side, wanting to get out of the way of the people sliding to a stop behind him. He pulled off his goggles and turned back, squinting up the path he'd just traversed. Even from this distance, The Lodge was a huge complex snugged up against the steep rock face of the mountain. But despite its size, the building didn't look out of place. Whoever had designed the hotel had taken pains to make the exterior blend in well with its surroundings. The whole complex looked like a natural extension of the wilderness, as if it was trying not to disturb the area.

Somewhere up there was Molly's office. Was she sitting at her desk, typing away on her computer? Or was she standing by a window, lost in thought as she gazed down the mountain?

He smiled at the thought that maybe, just maybe, they were looking at each other right now.

Max hadn't managed to fall asleep until the stars had begun to fade from the sky. He'd spent most of the night tossing and turning, his mind playing an endless loop of last evening's events. Dinner had been quite enjoyable, almost surprisingly so. He'd invited Molly over because he'd been attracted to her after their first meeting, but he hadn't expected to have such chemistry with her. She was so easy to talk to; she was one of those rare people who actually *listened*, rather than simply waiting for her turn to speak. It was a refreshing change from the conversations he was used to having with potential donors. He hadn't had to feign interest in subjects that he found boring, hadn't had to laugh at lame jokes. They'd been able to move beyond superficial niceties and actually start to get to know each other.

And then he'd messed it all up by pawing at her like a hormonal teenage boy.

He hadn't meant to make her uncomfortable. Hadn't intended to overstep her boundaries. He'd simply misread the signs. The kiss had short-circuited his brain, fogging up his normal clear-sightedness when it came to reading people.

He'd never forget the way Molly had stiffened under his hand. Embarrassment filled him at the memory, and his stomach churned. Max prided himself on being a man who made sure the women he was with enjoyed themselves with no regrets. But last night he had come across as a creep.

Molly had been gracious about accepting his apology. Still, it had been a disappointing way to end their evening.

But the worst part of all? How much he'd enjoyed kissing and touching her. He felt like a starving man who'd been given a taste of a scrumptious feast, only to have it jerked away after the first bite. A year was a long time to go without even a casual relationship, but between K-9 Cadets and his other responsibilities, the dearth of female companionship in his life hadn't really bothered him.

Now, though? He felt the void acutely. Last night's dinner and subsequent kiss had been like a wake-up call, a heady reminder of what it felt like to really connect with a woman. And while he understood there was no real future for him and Molly thanks to the geographical distance between them, he still wanted to make sure he didn't leave her with a bad impression.

He glanced at his watch. He was due to meet Blaine for a late lunch in an hour. Maybe he could ask his old friend about Molly? After all, the two of them were cousins. Blaine had to know something about her.

Max dismissed the thought almost immediately. Molly had been very clear yesterday that she didn't mix business and pleasure. That meant she would probably not appreciate Max talking about their dinner with Blaine. The two of them might be related, but they also worked together. The last thing Max wanted was for Molly to get any grief over seeing a guest on a social basis.

Still, there were other ways he could reach out to Molly without making her feel like she had to respond to his overture.

He walked over to the ski lift, pulled out his phone and took a seat on the moving chair. A few clicks later, he'd found exactly what he was looking for...

# Chapter 5

In what was staring to become a habit, Molly once again found herself knocking on the door to Max's cabin.

*This is crazy*, she told herself. But she needed to see him.

The flowers had arrived at her office a few hours ago. She'd been working on a project when a knock at the door had interrupted her concentration. She'd looked up to see a veritable wall of flowers filling her doorway. From somewhere out in the hall, a voice had called out, "Molly Gilford?"

The arrangement was gorgeous, a garden's worth of red roses, pink hydrangeas, white daffodils and sprays of yellow freesia. It took up all the space on the small side table in her office, and made the room smell like a perfumer's workshop. She'd never seen such an extravagant arrangement before, much less been the recipient of anything like it.

It had taken some searching to find the card, tucked away amid the blooms. Given the scope of the flowers, Molly figured they had to be from one of her corporate clients; she'd facilitated a retreat for a major airline last week, so this was probably a thank-you gift for her efforts.

She couldn't have been more wrong.

The typed message inside the card had been simple and sweet:

*Thanks for putting up with me last night.—Mike.*

Molly frowned at the unexpected signature. Was Max trying to be funny?

She pulled up his reservation information, curious to find if Mike was perhaps his middle name. But he'd registered as Maxwell Hollick; there was no middle initial.

Her gaze drifted over the flowers as she pondered this small mystery. Her cheeks heated as she sniffed one of the roses. Red roses meant passion; she knew that. A quick internet search helped her decode the meaning of the other blooms: romance, new beginnings and friendship.

Pleasure blossomed in her chest as she savored this new information. Did Max know the meanings of the flowers he'd chosen? Or had he simply told the florist to create a display?

Her thoughts returned to their conversation last night. Max was a smart man who seemed to know exactly what he wanted and how to go about getting it. This wasn't a typical arrangement—she'd never seen this combination of flowers before. Given what she knew about Max, it was likely he'd been very specific with the florist.

Which meant this subtle message wasn't a coincidence.

Molly leaned back in her chair, trying to decide how she felt about that.

There was no point in denying she found him attractive. If these flowers were any indication, Max felt the same way. But should she act on her desire?

*It's not smart*, whispered a small voice in her head. There were a myriad of reasons why exploring her attraction to Max was a bad idea.

Still, as she tallied up the risks, she couldn't help but wonder if she should throw caution to the wind and dive in anyway.

Her gaze drifted over the framed pictures on her desk. There was one of her with her siblings, and a formal portrait her parents had taken on their fortieth wedding anniversary. Seeing the photo reminded her of some advice her dad had given her several years ago.

"Molly," he'd said, "five years from now, what are you going to regret more? Doing this, or not doing it?"

He'd been right then, and he was right now. His words were the perfect litmus test for the major decisions in her life, including this one.

The answer came as soon as she considered the

question. Despite all the risks, all of the reasons it was a bad idea, she knew she'd regret passing up the opportunity to know Max better.

One question remained, though; with all the thought Max had put into this delivery, why was the card signed Mike?

Maybe he was trying to be discreet? He had to know such a fancy display of flowers in her office would attract attention. Perhaps he'd used the name so that anyone who saw the card wouldn't connect him with the gift. She had made a big deal about not dating guests, so this could be his way of keeping their date last night a secret.

She'd reached for the phone, intending to call his cabin and thank him. Then she'd thought better of the idea. This was a grand gesture. It deserved more than a phone call.

So as soon as she'd finished work, she'd grabbed the card and hiked up the trail to Max's cabin, hoping to solve the "Mike" mystery once and for all.

She knocked, stomping her feet on the mat to help ward off the chill. *Is he even here?* She hadn't bothered to call before setting out. Now, as the cold settled over her, she began to wonder if she'd made a mistake.

Another knock, but still no answer. Disappointment roiled in her stomach as she turned to leave. Now that Molly had made up her mind to embrace the chemistry she felt with Max, she didn't want to waste any of the time he had left at The Lodge. But

it seemed she would have to wait to thank him another time.

She was about ten feet down the trail when a furry
form shot past her and skidded to a stop on the path
ahead. Molly froze, a burst of adrenaline making
her heart pound as she squinted in the fading light.
Bears and mountain lions were generally shy crea-
tures, but they were more active at dusk. Every once
in a while, there was a sighting on the trails that connected the cabins to the main building. Was this the
latest incident?

Molly slowly took a step back, her brain whirl-
ing as she desperately tried to recall the safety training every employee was required to complete. Was
she supposed to drop to the ground and play dead?
Charge forward screaming? Or move away as calmly
as possible?

The creature took a step forward. Molly's throat
tightened as she suppressed a scream. Just as she
took another step back, a voice cut through the air.

"Furbert? Dammit, dog, where are you?"

Molly saw the animal start to wag its tail. She
took a deep breath, her panic fading as the dog trotted over and she got a good look at him.

He stopped at her feet and plopped his butt on the
ground, staring up at her expectantly.

"Furbert?" Max called out again.

"He's here," she said. She knew from experience
Max probably couldn't see them in the gloaming, and
she didn't want him to worry about his dog.

Max was quiet for a second. Molly imagined he

was frowning, trying to place her voice. Then he spoke again. "Molly?"

She smiled at his tone, a mix of pleasure and surprise. "The one and only."

Molly heard the crunch of shoes on the gravelly trail. Then Max stood next to her, looking down with a grin. "This is a nice surprise," he said.

Her heart started to pound again, though not from fear. She stared up at him, thrilled to be close to him once more.

He was wearing glasses, a simple pair of black frames that should have made him look nerdy. On him, though, they were sexy. "Hello," she stammered, feeling suddenly self-conscious. Why hadn't she brushed her hair or put on lipstick before coming out here?

"What's going on?" Before she could reply, he shivered and hugged himself. He wasn't wearing a coat, only jeans and a sweatshirt. The sun had all but disappeared, and cold came early on the mountain. "Actually, scratch that. Do you mind if we talk inside? I'm not used to this weather."

Molly nodded, all too happy to get out of the growing darkness. Even though the blurry shape had turned out to be Furbert, there was a primitive part of her brain that was still reeling from the scare. Shelter was a good choice, at least until her body relaxed again.

They started walking toward the cabin. Max snapped his fingers, which was apparently the only signal Furbert needed to follow his master. He held the door open for her, and Molly walked past him and into the soothing warmth of the living room.

"So what are you doing out here?" Max asked as he shut the door. "Not that I'm not happy to see you. But I wasn't expecting you."

Molly moved to stand in front of the fire blazing at the hearth in the corner of the living room. "I should have called first. I came by to say thank you, but it didn't seem like you were here."

Max plucked at the cord of the earbuds dangling around his neck. "I was listening to music while I got some work done. I didn't hear you knock, but Furbert did. He kept scratching at the door. When I went to let him out, he took off like a shot."

"I'm glad he didn't run into the woods," Molly said. "Believe it or not, we have bears and mountain lions up here. I'd hate for him to get hurt."

"Oh, he's not the type to roam," Max reassured her. "He just wanted to get to you."

As if to prove his master's point, Furbert walked over to the fireplace and sat at Molly's feet. She reached down to scratch behind his ears, earning a contented sigh for her efforts.

"But enough about him," Max said. "Have a seat." He gestured to the sofa. "Can I get you something to drink?"

Molly shook her head as she walked over to the couch. She settled onto the cushion, in the same spot she had occupied last night. Max sat next to her, angling his body toward hers.

"Like I said, I came by to thank you."

Warmth glowed in his eyes. "Did you like the flowers?"

"Oh, yes." She got out her phone, showed him a few of the pictures she'd taken of the arrangement. "They're gorgeous. I've never seen anything like them."

Max glanced at her photos, then back to her. "Looks like the florist did a nice job."

"They did," she agreed. "But it does seem like someone else is trying to take credit for your work." She reached into her bag, pulled out the card. "Who exactly is Mike?"

Max read the message with a frown. "Unbelievable," he muttered. He shook his head, chuckling softly. "When I dictated the message for the card, I wanted it to be signed as just *M.* I didn't want to put my name, in case someone saw it. So to make it clear, I said '*M* as in Mike,' which is the military designation for the letter." He handed the card back to her, clearly amused. "I guess the person on the other end of the line just heard 'Mike.'"

"Well, that clears things up," Molly said. "But I must say, I was rather hoping you were a secret agent or something."

Max threw back his head, laughter pouring out of him. The sound wrapped around her like a velvet rope, making her want to get closer to him.

"I'm afraid I'm not that interesting," he said. "Sorry to disappoint you."

"I'll get over it," she retorted, unable to keep from smiling.

Max settled back against the arm of the sofa, watching her face. "I'm glad you liked the flowers. It was the least I could do."

Molly tilted her head to the side. "What do you mean by that?" Why did it seem like he was trying to apologize?

Max glanced down. "Last night." He sounded almost shy. "I made you uncomfortable when I kissed you."

What was he talking about? Molly racked her brain, trying to figure out what she'd done to give him that impression.

Then it hit her. "Oh," she said slowly. She'd stiffened when he'd touched her, and now that she thought about it, that had been the moment he had stopped kissing her. He'd also apologized before going to get her coat. "I told you last night, I'm not upset with you."

He glanced up at her, interest sharpening his gaze. "You aren't?"

Molly shook her head. "Hardly."

"But...you tensed up."

"I was surprised, that's all." She debated if she should say more, then decided to forge ahead. "I haven't dated anyone in a while," she confessed, reaching out to pet Furbert, who had relocated to sit at her feet once more. "I'd forgotten how nice it feels to be touched that way."

He didn't reply. As the silence stretched between them, Molly realized she shouldn't have said anything. Max probably felt sorry for her, which was the last thing she wanted.

*Well done*, she thought sarcastically. With only a few words, she'd managed to throw a wet blanket over the chemistry smoldering between them.

Time to go. She glanced down, wondering how she was going to stand up with the dog practically sitting on her feet. He looked quite comfortable, but he was just going to have to move.

She planted one hand on the couch to push off the cushion. But before she could shift her weight, Max covered her hand with his own.

Molly looked over, surprised by the gesture.

He had leaned in when she wasn't looking, closing some of the distance between them. His soft green eyes looked almost golden as they reflected the light from the fire. Molly felt hypnotized by his gaze, unable to move, unable to look away.

He lifted her hand, turning it over to fit in the cradle of his palm. Using the tip of his index finger, he began to softly trace the lines of her palm. His touch was featherlight, hardly more than a brush of skin against skin. But it sent electric currents of sensation shooting up her arm with every stroke.

"Do you know what I missed the most while I was on deployment?"

The question came out of left field, but his voice was so quiet it didn't break the mood building between them. Molly swallowed, her mind growing hazy even as her body stood at attention.

"No," she said softly. "What?"

"Touching someone. Being touched in return." He looked down at her hand, continuing to trace imaginary patterns on her skin. "Not always in a sexual way, either. There's just something about physical contact that soothes the soul, don't you think?"

Molly nodded, falling completely under his spell. "It does." She'd never tried to articulate it before, but Max's words perfectly described her feelings.

"I'm glad I didn't upset you last night," he said gruffly. "I worried about it all day."

"You did?" She was surprised by his admission. Max seemed so confident and sure of himself—not the type to fret about a small misstep. His concern warmed her just as much as the fire a few feet away.

He nodded. "But since I didn't overstep my bounds, does that mean I can kiss you again?"

The question sent a thrill through her, kicking her heart rate up a notch. "I take it you want to kiss me?" Yes, she was teasing him. But the anticipation was so enjoyable, Molly wanted to make it last just a little bit longer…

"Oh, yes." His eyes dipped to her mouth, then back up again. "If you don't mind too much." The corner of his mouth quirked up in a smile, letting her know he was in on the game, as well.

She leaned over, getting closer to him. "That might be nice," she whispered. "I just need to check my calendar."

Max angled his head, putting them only a breath apart. "Busy, are you?"

Molly smiled. "Mmm. But I think I can pencil you in."

She closed the distance between them, fitting her mouth over his. Just as it had last night, the contact sent sparks of sensation shooting through her system.

Max wasted no time pulling her closer. Her curves pressed against the flat planes of his body, a delicious pressure that sharpened her need for more.

They explored each other's mouths, tongues and lips communicating more than words ever could. Molly gave herself over to the sheer pleasure of the kiss, the voice of doubt that constantly whispered in her brain silenced for the time being.

After a moment, Max pulled back, though he didn't go far. He pressed his forehead to hers, breathing hard. "That was..." He trailed off.

"Intense," Molly finished.

"Yeah." He huffed out a laugh, his hand gently stroking her cheek.

"Don't stop on my account," she said, only half-joking.

"Really?" He drew back farther, his eyes scanning her face as if searching for signs of uncertainty.

She smiled and nodded. "Really," she assured him. As soon as she said the word, the rest of her doubts faded away. They might not have a future together, but she didn't want to pass up the chance to fully explore the chemistry between them. At least once in her life, Molly wanted to know what real passion felt like.

Max returned her smile. "Stay right there," he

said. Then he rose from the sofa and walked into the bedroom, leaving her alone.

Well, not entirely alone. Furbert took notice of Max's departure and hopped up onto the cushion next to her. He curled up at her side, placing his head in her lap, then looked up at her with a pitiful expression. It was a masterful performance; if Molly didn't know better, she'd swear he was starved for affection.

"All right," she said, stifling a laugh. She scratched behind his ears, and he sighed blissfully again.

She was glad Furbert was here. Petting him was a nice distraction while she awaited Max's return. If she'd been left alone with her thoughts, her nerves might have gotten the better of her.

It didn't take long for Max to come back into the living room. He had ditched the glasses, and the earbuds no longer dangled around his neck. His hair was slightly mussed, making her think he'd run his hand through it. "Oh, I see how it is," he joked. "I'm gone for five minutes and you've already moved on to the next man."

Molly shrugged. "I told you my calendar was full."

He ran his hand down Furbert's back. "Mind if I steal her away, boy?"

Furbert's tail thumped against the cushion, but he didn't move.

"Come on," Max said affectionately. "Go lie down by the fire."

The dog let out a dramatic sigh as he got to his

feet and jumped down. Molly couldn't help but laugh at his antics. "Does he always complain this much?"

"Pretty much," Max said. "He's like an old man." He held out his hand. Molly took it, experiencing a second of déjà vu as he helped her to her feet.

"Would you like some wine?" he offered.

Molly shook her head. "Not right now." She wanted to be clearheaded for what came next. That way, when she thought back to this encounter, she'd remember everything in detail.

He drew her into the bedroom, and she immediately saw why he'd left her on the couch.

The bedroom was large, with a king-size bed on the far wall. The entrance to the bathroom was on the left, and the wall of windows on the right ended in a corner fireplace with a small sitting area arranged to take advantage of the view.

Max had lit the fire, casting the room in a golden glow. The chairs and small table were pushed to the side, and Max had pulled the quilts off the bed and placed them in front of the fire. Pillows were arranged on the makeshift pallet, creating a cozy little nest.

"Is this okay?" He sounded a bit unsure as he studied her face. "I thought it might be nice to lie by the fire, but if you'd rather not be on the floor I can put everything back on the bed."

"No, this is perfect," Molly said. She'd never made love by a fire before. It was one of those romantic scenes she'd always wanted to experience but figured she never would. The men she'd been with in the past had been nice, but not especially interested in setting the mood. Max's thoughtfulness made her feel special, as if she were the only woman in the world.

He pulled her close. "I'm glad you think so." He pressed a soft kiss to her lips, then her nose. "This isn't something I want to rush." He kissed one cheek, then the other. "I plan on enjoying our time together." His lips met her forehead. "I want you to, as well." He placed his index finger under her chin and tipped her head back to expose her neck. His lips were hot against the sensitive skin along her jaw.

Molly shivered with pleasure. "I will," she managed to choke out. Her body already ached for his, though he'd hardly touched her.

He slanted his lips over hers, cupping her face with his hands as he explored her mouth. Molly found the hem of his sweatshirt. She tugged blindly at it, seeking access to his skin.

Max jumped when she touched him. "Sorry," he muttered with a laugh. "I'm a little ticklish."

His admission delighted her. A Green Beret who was afraid of spiders and ticklish to boot? It was an unlikely combination.

"That's going to make things…interesting." How was she going to touch him without torturing him?

"It's just along my sides," he said, running his fingers down her ribs. His nimble fingers unbuttoned her blouse. Molly shrugged out of it, letting it drop to the floor.

Max traced the line of her collarbone. "I'm not ticklish here," he murmured. His hand drifted down the swell of her breasts. "Or here." He ran the knuckle of his forefinger across the curve of her stomach. "Or here."

Molly swallowed, trying to bring some moisture back into her dry mouth. "That's good to know." She practically panted out the words. "But I can't just take your word for it. I'm going to need to test that out for myself."

Max nodded, his expression serious. "Trust but verify. I get it." He winked at her, then took a half step back and pulled his sweatshirt over his head.

Molly sighed with appreciation as she surveyed his body. The firelight cast flickering shadows on his upper torso, a terrain her fingers itched to explore.

She stepped closer, placing her palms flat on his chest. He was warm and solid against her hands, the red-gold smattering of hair surprisingly soft.

He remained still while she ran her fingers over him, indulging her curiosity as she wandered the planes of his torso. She felt the thump of his heart against his breastbone, noticed the change in rhythm when she dipped her head forward and flicked one nipple with the tip of her tongue.

Max sucked in his breath with a hiss as she moved her hands down, following the vertical line of hair that bisected his stomach to disappear behind the waistband of his pants. She reached for the button of his jeans, but stopped when he grabbed her hands.

"It's my turn," he rasped, lifting her hands and placing them on his shoulders.

Molly nodded. "Fair enough."

He traced the edges of her bra with his fingertip, then dipped his head and navigated the same path with his tongue. His breath was hot on her skin, a second caress that made her knees wobble.

He reached for the front clasp of her bra, fumbling a bit as he tried to unhook it. Molly reached down, intending to help him. But he shook his head. "I've got it," he said, gently lifting her hands to his shoulders once more.

A second later, her bra loosened, releasing her breasts into his hands. Max hummed appreciatively as he rubbed the pads of his thumbs over her nipples. Molly's knees turned to jelly, forcing her to tighten her grip on his shoulders so she didn't fall to the ground.

Max kissed her, slowly lowering her to the floor as he did. Molly was all too happy to follow his lead— her brain was overwhelmed by the fog of arousal, making thought difficult.

The comforter was a soft cushion under her back, though he could have stretched her out on a bed of nails and she wouldn't have noticed. The fire chased the chill from the room, but it was nothing compared to the heat of Max's body on top of hers. He was like a living furnace, warming her from the inside out with his touch.

She shifted, reaching for the button on his pants once more. He pushed himself up, meeting her eyes. "Are you certain?"

Molly nodded, afraid to speak lest she shout, "God, yes!"

Max rolled to the side and shucked his pants. Molly followed suit by lifting her hips to shove her trousers and panties down her legs. When they were both free, they rolled to face each other again.

Molly skimmed her hand across his chest and down his stomach, until she reached her goal. She traced the length of him, enjoying the tension in his muscles as he sucked in a breath.

"Two can play that game," he murmured wickedly. His fingers started at her knee and stroked up the inside of her thigh. Then his hand cupped her center, where the sensitive tissues responded to the smallest of movements.

Max played her body like a musical instrument. Their connection was unlike anything Molly had experienced before. He seemed to know exactly where to touch her, how to stroke and nip and lick and kiss. There were times she felt he must be reading her mind—how else could she explain the intensity of this experience?

She let go of any pretense of control, surrendering to her body's responses. For the first time in her life, Molly silenced the voice of self-consciousness in her head and got out of the way of her own pleasure. She didn't think about what she looked like, or worry that she was too curvy or too plain or too *anything* for Max. She simply jettisoned the self-doubt and let herself *feel*.

From somewhere in the distance, she heard the crinkle of a wrapper. "Oh, good," she murmured. "You have protection."

"I do," he confirmed. "It's taken care of."

He kissed her again. Molly reached for him, pulling him on top of her. She drew her legs up, letting her knees fall apart. Max entered her carefully, giving her time to adjust as he pushed forward. She bit her lip, moaning softly. It felt incredible to be connected to him, for their bodies to be joined completely in this primal way.

Her release came quickly, waves of pleasure washing over her with an intensity that made her see stars. Max found his completion soon after, his muscles flexing under her hands. He relaxed, slowly settling his weight on top of her. Molly idly ran her hand up and down his back, enjoying the feel of being surrounded by him.

She wasn't sure how long they lay there like that—her brain was pleasantly empty of all thoughts, a slate wiped clean. At some point, Max rolled onto his back. Without saying a word, he gathered her close. Molly snuggled up next to him, resting her head on his shoulder. She threw her arm across his chest, feeling the thump of his heart as the rhythm returned to normal.

Max's hand traced imaginary patterns on her upper arm, a lazy caress that lulled Molly into a stupor. "That was amazing," he said softly, his voice a low rumble that she felt as much as heard.

"Yeah," she murmured. There was more she wanted to say, but her brain was still flying high from pleasure, which made it difficult to think. She stared at the fire, transfixed by the dance of the dying flames.

Max grabbed the edge of the comforter and pulled the thick material across their legs to ward off the cold. "Can you stay the night?" he asked.

His question made her heart want to sing. "Yes," she said.

"Good." He gave her a squeeze, then relaxed again. "We can get into bed eventually. I just don't think I can move now."

Molly chuckled. Once again, they were on the same page. "This is nice," she said on a sigh. "I'm in no rush."

The fire crackled a few feet away, the occasional spark popping in a bright flare that reminded her of a shooting star. Max's breath was even and regular in her ear, his skin warm against her cheek. Sleep reached for her with welcoming arms, and she surrendered to its embrace with a sigh.

# Chapter 6

*Present day*

Max knew the instant Molly woke, even though he couldn't see her face. She stiffened in his arms, and a slight hitch interrupted her deep, regular breathing.

She didn't speak, but he could practically feel her confusion as she lifted her head off his chest, peering into the dark gondola carriage as she no doubt tried to get her bearings.

"It's okay," he said softly. "We're still in the gondola."

She shivered, pushing up and out of his arms. He let her go, his body instantly registering the cold as she left his embrace.

"How long have we been here?"

"Almost six hours," he said. "The team said they're getting close. Shouldn't be too much longer now." Hopefully that was the truth. He knew the rescuers were working hard to reach them. But there were a lot of factors outside their control, limiting the speed with which they could operate. Fortunately, the gondola carriage seemed to be stable, if cold. As long as things stayed that way, they could wait a while longer.

Molly rubbed her eyes. "How long was I out?"

"Almost two hours."

"Oh, man." She sighed, shook her head. "I'm sorry. I didn't mean to fall asleep. And certainly not on you."

"No need to apologize." He didn't tell her it had been the best two hours he'd spent in a long time.

Holding Molly had kept him from going out of his mind with boredom. Despite the swell of her belly, she'd fit against him perfectly. As soon as she'd nodded off, he'd gathered her into his arms, their bodies coming together in a pose they'd adopted a hundred times before. How many times had they slept like this, wrapped in each other's arms?

Molly was the only woman he'd really held before. Beth hadn't liked to be touched while she slept, so every night they'd retreated to separate sides of the bed, leaving a gulf of space between them. Max had figured he wouldn't be able to sleep any other way, but from the very start he'd always felt more contented with Molly in his arms. Just the weight of her against him brought him peace.

He'd been amazed to find that was still the case. Her earlier burst of anger at his lack of communication had made her seem like a bit of a stranger, and pregnancy had changed her body in ways he didn't recognize. He'd spent most of the time trying to wrap his brain around the fact that as he held her, their baby was cradled between them.

But in spite of all those changes, one thing remained constant: Molly still smelled the same. He'd taken one whiff of her hair and the months of separation had melted away, making him feel as though he'd seen her only yesterday.

Things were different between them, that much was sure. But holding Molly had made him think everything might turn out all right after all.

Provided they got out of here in one piece.

He reached for his phone, wincing a bit as the movement pulled his shoulder.

"Still hurts?" Molly asked.

"It's fine," he said.

She eyed him doubtfully. "I think you're going to need a little more than ice and ibuprofen."

He didn't want to talk about his shoulder, didn't want her to worry about him. "How's your head?" In the gray light of the carriage, he could see that a dark bruise had formed at the edge of her hair. Even though she hadn't hit her belly in the earlier commotion, he'd feel better once she'd been seen by a doctor.

"I've been better," she admitted. "I just want to go home and take a hot bath."

"I'm going to call the fire department again." Impatience bubbled in Max's chest. "We need to get you out of here."

As he thumbed through the call history on his phone, a low hum filled the air. It grew steadily louder, resolving into the characteristic *thwop-thwop-thwop* of a helicopter blade.

Max reflexively glanced up, though he couldn't see through the ceiling of the gondola. "That might be our ride," he murmured.

Sure enough, the sound kept growing louder until it reached a crescendo over their heads. Molly looked nervous. "I probably should have asked this before," she said loudly. "But how exactly are they going to get us down?"

"It depends," Max replied. There were a couple of possibilities—they could rappel down to the ground, or be pulled into the body of the helicopter and ride to safety. Given Molly's inexperience with rope lines and the state of his shoulder, Max sincerely hoped the rescuers opted for the latter option.

Loud thumps sounded on the roof of the carriage. Metal groaned as the rescuers on the roof pried open the hatch of the carriage. A blast of cold air entered the space, and Max drew Molly close to try to keep her warm. A metal ladder descended from the hatch. Max helped guide it to the floor, then stepped back to make room for the rescuers.

The first man descended the ladder quickly. Once inside the carriage, he pushed his ski goggles onto his forehead and glanced around. His eyes landed on Molly, and he smiled broadly.

"Hello, ma'am. My name is John, and I'll be your rescue worker today."

He was a big man, at least five inches taller than Max. Long legs, broad shoulders, muscled arms and a dark beard completed the picture. *Like a lumberjack straight out of central casting*, Max thought sourly. All that was missing were the flannel shirt and ax.

John's size made Max feel a bit inadequate, and it didn't help that Molly was staring up at him like he was some kind of superhero.

*Stop it*, he told himself. The only thing that mattered right now was getting her to safety. The fact that her rescuer had a pretty face shouldn't bother him. John was just going to get her out of the gondola—nothing more.

John nodded at him. "My partner will take care of you, sir," he said. He glanced up. "Hey, Chris. Plenty of room in here for you to join us."

A second man climbed down the ladder. He was closer to Max's height and build, and had the look of a ski bum. "Howdy," he said.

"Hello," Max replied. "So how are we going to do this? Up or down?"

"Up," said John. "The wind is starting to pick up again, and we don't want you folks sliding down ropes in case it turns nasty."

Max nodded in agreement. It would be a lot easier for Molly to ride in the helicopter, and they wouldn't have to worry about getting off the side of the mountain after making it to the ground.

"What does that mean?" Molly asked, her worry plain.

Max opened his mouth to explain, but John beat him to it. "I'm going to put this harness on you, ma'am," he said, lifting the gear with one hand. "Then we're going to climb to the roof of the gondola, and the crew in the helicopter will winch us up."

Molly's cheeks went pale. "Okay."

"Don't worry," John said with a smile. "I'll be holding you the whole way."

Max fought the urge to roll his eyes. This guy was really laying it on thick. But Molly seemed to appreciate it.

"All right," she said, nodding. Her eyes widened as John stepped closer, harness in hand.

"Ready?" he asked.

"Sure," she said, her voice a little shaky.

Max clenched his jaw as he watched John's big hands move over Molly's body, tightening straps, securing buckles. *He* should be the one helping her, not this burly stranger.

"What about you?" Chris asked him.

Max reached for the harness and began to strap himself in, his eyes on Molly and John the whole time.

"I take it you've done this before?" Chris asked.

"Yeah. I'm former military," Max said, not really paying attention to Chris.

"Right on, brother," Chris said.

Max didn't reply. He was too busy staring holes

into John's back as the man knelt to arrange the straps between Molly's legs. He reached up to secure a belt around her stomach, but paused when Molly clutched her belly protectively.

John spoke softly, but Max was so focused on the pair of them that he heard him clearly. "Are you—?"

Molly nodded.

John patted her hip, causing Max to see red. "Don't worry," he said quietly. "I'll get you both out of here safely."

"Am I just going to be dangling from a rope?" Molly asked nervously.

"Not exactly," John said. He stood, towering over her. "I'm going to bend my knees, like I'm sitting." He walked over to the ladder, leaning against it as he demonstrated the pose he was going to assume. "You'll sit on my lap, facing me. Lock your ankles around my waist, and I'll keep my arms around you. I'll hold us steady as we go up."

Max thought his head might explode, but by some miracle, he managed to keep his emotions in check.

"First things first, though," John said. He shrugged out of his coat, revealing—*of course*, Max thought— a flannel shirt.

John draped his coat around Molly's shoulders, making Max feel like a giant ass. He wanted to protest, to let everyone know he'd offered her his sweater, but it hadn't fit.

"It's cold outside, and that wind is no joke," John said. "Don't want you turning into a Popsicle on the way up."

"Thanks," Molly said, smiling up at him. "I appreciate it."

"I don't think my coat will fit you," Chris said as he finished checking the fit of Max's harness. "But we have blankets in the chopper."

"No worries. I'll be fine," Max managed to grit out.

"Ladies first," John said, gesturing for Molly to start up the stairs.

She grabbed the first rung, but before she began to climb she glanced at Max. "Are you going to be okay with your shoulder?"

Both John and Chris turned to look at him. "Are you hurt, sir?" Chris asked, his gaze sharpening as he gave Max a once-over.

Max shrugged, wishing Molly hadn't said anything. He didn't want to look weak in front of these men. It was a ridiculous reaction, but he had his pride…

"We got tossed around a bit earlier," he said. "I wrenched my shoulder, but it's fine. I'll be okay for the ride up."

"All right," Chris said. "I know you're a pro, but I'll stand at your back and hold you steady. Will that work for you?"

Max nodded, knowing he couldn't really refuse. These men had safety protocols to follow, and the last thing he wanted was to make their job more difficult.

He watched as first Molly and then John ascended the ladder. Max scrambled up after John, his head popping through the hatch just in time to see Molly climb onto John's lap. She wrapped her legs around his waist and threw her arms around his neck, clinging to his large frame like a barnacle.

A wave of jealousy washed over Max, the emotion so strong he nearly lost his grip on the ladder. It should be *him* holding Molly like that, *him* rescuing her from the gondola. Instead, he had to watch while some stranger lifted his woman and unborn baby to safety.

Except…was she still his woman? Their relationship had been episodic at best, moments of stolen time he'd carved out of his schedule. They'd never made their association public, never let Blaine or anyone else know they were together. They only saw each other when he stayed at The Lodge during his quarterly visits. When Max considered things from a different perspective, their connection seemed like less of a relationship and more of an ongoing booty call.

The thought left a bad taste in his mouth. He'd never thought of their relationship in such cheap terms before. But as he watched Molly and John rise into the air, he had to wonder if perhaps his actions had made Molly feel that he took her for granted.

He certainly hadn't meant for her to feel…disposable. The problem was, he couldn't offer her anything permanent. After the demise of his first marriage, Max knew he wasn't a forever kind of guy.

But Molly was carrying his child. It didn't get more serious than that.

He relaxed a bit as she and John disappeared into

the body of the helicopter. Chris stepped behind him. "Our turn," he said loudly. Max nodded, ignoring the cold gusts of wind buffeting the gondola carriage.

Max felt a tug and then they were airborne, slowly moving away from the roof of the carriage. He knew he should look around, take advantage of the uninterrupted view. This was likely the last time he'd fly through the air without being encased by glass. But he couldn't take his eyes off the door of the helicopter.

Molly was up there, waiting for him. When they'd been stranded in the gondola, it had been easy to feel like life had hit the pause button. In some ways, he wished they'd had more time together, so they could have come to an understanding about how things stood between them. But now they were returning to reality, and they were no closer to knowing what to do next.

"Don't give up on me yet," he murmured. Max knew he didn't deserve a second chance after the way he had treated her, but maybe Molly would listen to him for the sake of their baby if nothing else. He didn't think they could ever go back to the way things had been between them, but there had to be something he could do to help them move forward, some plan he could devise to make things right again.

He had a goal. Now he just had to figure out how to reach it.

## Chapter 7

"Do you know how much longer this will take?"

Molly tugged the thin sheet over her legs, shifting a bit as she searched for a comfortable position. The hospital mattress was thin, and though both the head and foot of the bed were adjustable, she had yet to find an angle that didn't make her back hurt.

"I believe you're next on the list," said the nurse. "I'm sorry about the wait. It's been a little crazy around here."

Her words triggered a rush of guilt. "No, I'm sorry," Molly said. "I don't mean to complain. I know you guys are doing the best you can after the avalanche."

The woman gave her a grateful smile. "Let me bring you another blanket," she offered. "I know it's chilly in here, and you must still be cold after your ordeal."

"Thank you," she murmured as the nurse left.

Alone again, Molly rested her hand on her belly. The baby had been reassuringly active throughout the afternoon and into the evening. Even though she'd missed her ob-gyn appointment, the ER doctor had mentioned doing an ultrasound to make sure everything was okay. Maybe she'd get to find out the sex of the baby today after all...

Max's face flashed through her mind. Would he be here for the scan? More importantly, did she want him to be?

The helicopter ride down the mountain hadn't taken too long. John had sat beside her the whole time, a steady presence amid the rush of activity. Max had sat across from her, watching her quietly. Molly could tell there were things he wanted to say, but the noise inside the helicopter kept him from speaking. Then they'd landed, and each of them had been ushered into the back of separate waiting ambulances. She had no idea where he was now. Maybe he was still waiting to see a doctor, too. Or perhaps he'd already been treated and released.

If that was the case, would he wait for her? Or would he leave her here while he made his way back to The Lodge, where Furbert was undoubtedly waiting for him?

At the moment, Molly wasn't sure which option she preferred. Given his reaction in the gondola, it was clear he wasn't happy about the baby. She knew he was still adjusting to the news, but if he was going to ultimately decide to leave, she'd rather he did it now. If he stuck around to try out the role of father and supportive partner, it would hurt all the more if and when he decided the job just wasn't for him. Besides, her baby deserved more than a part-time dad.

But could Max really offer more? He was totally devoted to his charity, a fact that had seemed admirable before. Now it made her wonder if there was room in his life for anything else. He had a track record of prioritizing his work over his personal life. She recalled him telling her about his marriage, the way his commitment to the team had placed a lot of strain on the relationship and ultimately contributed to his divorce. He'd since thrown himself into K-9 Cadets, pushing everything else in his life to the fringes.

Including her.

Molly couldn't find it in her to be bitter, though. She'd known the score when she'd first gotten involved with him. And while she'd accepted the fact that Max didn't think their relationship could move beyond their quarterly visits, she wasn't willing to consign her child to the same fate. Their baby deserved to have center stage in Max's life.

But would he agree?

She didn't know what kind of history Max had with his own father—he'd never talked about his parents with her before. Now she wondered what kind of childhood he'd had, and what kind of upbringing he wanted for his own kids.

It was one of many conversations they needed to have in the coming days. If Max held true to pattern, however, he would only be in town for the week. They were going to have to pack a lot of decisions into that short period of time, which meant Molly needed to try to keep an open mind. After Max's radio silence in response to her messages, she'd just about accepted the idea of being a single mother; now she had to allow for the possibility that Max would want to coparent their baby.

A soft rap sounded on the door; probably the nurse returning with the extra blanket. Molly called out, "Come in," just as the door was pushed open a crack.

Max peered into the room. "Hi."

"Hi." Relief was a warm rush in her chest, though she quickly quashed the emotion. He was here now, sure. But she couldn't read too much into that. There was still plenty of time for him to walk away.

"May I come in?" He sounded hesitant, which was a departure from his usual confidence.

"Sure."

He slipped inside, revealing a sling on his left arm.

"Are you okay?" she asked as he settled into the chair by her bed.

"What, this?" He lifted his arm slightly. "Yeah, it's okay. Just a little strain."

"Let me guess," she said drily. "They told you to ice it and take ibuprofen?"

He grinned, "Right you are. I tried to save them the trouble, but they insisted on the sling."

Molly rolled her eyes. "You're not a Green Beret anymore. It's okay to be human."

"Never," he deadpanned, leaning back in the chair. "What about you? How's your head?"

"Fine. Just a bump." The doctor who had initially examined her had cleaned a little blood off the spot, but had declared she didn't need stitches. Molly had passed some kind of concussion screen, and the woman had told her to rest and take over-the-counter medication for any pain she might develop.

"What about the baby?"

"I think everything is okay there, too, but I'm waiting for an ultrasound."

Max nodded, absorbing this information. "Um… do you mind if I stay for that?" He looked simultaneously guarded and hopeful, as if he wanted to stay but was prepared to accept no for an answer.

"Yes, you can stay," Molly said. She was glad he actually wanted to be there for the scan, though perhaps he needed to see the baby to truly believe this was happening.

They sat in silence for a moment. "I'm surprised you're still here," she commented. "I figured you'd leave after being seen to get back to Furbert."

"I'm sure he's fine," Max said. "I managed to get ahold of Blaine, who said none of the cabins were affected by the avalanche. I left out food and water, so he should be good for a while."

Molly was glad to hear it. Furbert really was a sweet dog, and she'd hate for anything to happen to him.

There was another rap on the door, and this time a doctor entered, pulling a rolling cart after him. "Hi there," he said, his tone friendly. "I'm Dr. Fitzpatrick, the OB on call tonight. Just going to do a quick scan to make sure the baby is all right."

"Sounds good," Molly said.

Dr. Fitzpatrick eyed Max as he set up the ultrasound. "Are you the baby's father?"

Max's eyes widened slightly. "Yes," he replied. Molly thought she heard a hint of surprise in his voice, as if he didn't quite believe he was really here.

"Great, great," Dr. Fitzpatrick said as he pushed buttons and twisted knobs. He turned to Molly. "Ready for the goo?"

Molly smiled wryly. "I suppose."

"It's warm," the doctor assured her. "I wouldn't give you cold stuff."

"Thanks." She tugged up the gown, and Dr. Fitzpatrick tucked a sheet across her hips. Then he applied a healthy dollop of gel to her abdomen; true to his word, it was pleasantly warm on her skin.

"Here we go," he said. He applied the wand to her belly. After a few seconds, a steady *thump-thump-thump* filled the air.

"Is that—?" Max leaned forward, his expression rapt as he stared at the grainy images on the screen.

"The heartbeat, yes," Dr. Fitzpatrick said. "Nice and strong." He made a few notations on the screen, and a number popped up. "One hundred fifty beats per minute—that's perfect."

Molly smiled, the last of the tension draining from

her body. She'd been fairly certain the baby was okay, but it felt good to have it confirmed for sure.

"You've got a wiggle worm in here," Dr. Fitzpatrick commented, moving the wand over her belly. "Lots of movement."

"Is that okay?" Max's voice was closer now. Molly glanced over to find him standing by the bed now, his seat abandoned.

"Oh, yes. We like to see that," the doctor replied.

"Is there any way you can tell if it's a boy or a girl?" Molly asked. "I was supposed to find out today."

"I can try," the doctor answered. "Let's see if this little one will cooperate." He moved the wand around, showing them arms, legs, hands and feet. "That's the heart," he said. "Here's the stomach."

Molly felt Max grab her hand, but she was too fascinated by the images on the screen to look at him. "Here are the baby's kidneys, and this little dark spot is the amniotic fluid in the stomach."

"The fluid is inside the baby?" Max sounded confused and a little worried.

Dr. Fitzpatrick nodded. "At this stage, babies are practicing their swallowing skills. They swallow the amniotic fluid, which helps their gut to develop."

"My God," Max murmured, clearly amazed.

"Here's the brain—all the bits are there," the doctor continued. "And now let me try...yep, there we go." He clicked something, freezing the picture on the screen. "There's your answer."

"Okay," Max said slowly. "Can you help me out a little here? What are we looking at?"

"It's more a matter of what you're *not* looking at," the doctor explained.

"It's a girl," Molly said softly. She glanced at Dr. Fitzpatrick for confirmation. "Right?"

He nodded, seeming pleased she had figured it out. "Yes, indeed. You're having a baby girl."

A surge of emotion surged through Molly, making her eyes well up with tears. She hadn't thought it was possible to feel more love for the baby in her womb, but in that moment, her heart seemed to grow even larger. "A girl," she whispered, barely able to speak past her happiness.

She glanced up at Max, hoping to share some of the joy of this moment with him. He was as pale as a ghost, his wide eyes fixed on the screen. "A girl," he said a little hoarsely.

Dr. Fitzpatrick smiled. "Congratulations," he murmured. "I have two daughters myself. I can confirm girls are a lot of fun."

Max nodded mechanically, but Molly could tell he wasn't really hearing the doctor. "A girl," he repeated to himself.

The doctor eyed Max, then turned to Molly with an amused look. "It seems the news comes as a bit of a shock."

"In more ways than one." Molly sniffed, dabbing at her eyes with the sheet. "But he'll adjust." And if he didn't? She'd have no problem showing him the door.

She leaned back against the pillow, a dreamy smile on her face as the doctor wiped the gel off her belly.

"Everything looks good to me," Dr. Fitzpatrick said. "Follow up with your regular doctor in a couple of days, but I see nothing to worry about. Congratulations to you both."

"Thank you," Molly said, unable to contain her grin.

"Thanks," Max echoed woodenly.

Dr. Fitzpatrick wheeled the ultrasound machine out of the room. As soon as the door closed behind him, Max sank back into the chair. He looked positively shell-shocked, staring off into space though clearly seeing nothing.

Molly studied him a moment, trying to give him a little time to process the news. "What do you think?"

"Hmm?" he said absently.

"I asked you what you think," she repeated, not bothering to keep the edge from her tone. "You don't seem happy about the news the baby is a girl."

Max shook his head. "No, it's not that. It's just…" He trailed off, still staring into space. "I haven't thought about kids in a long time—not since the early days of my marriage. And even then, when I did think about them, it never occurred to me I might have a girl."

It seemed her earlier fears had been correct. Max wasn't interested in children. And now that they knew the sex of the baby, he could use that as another excuse to walk away.

"I'm sorry to disappoint you," she choked out. Tears filled her eyes again, but in sorrow this time.

"I didn't say I was disappointed," he said quietly. "Just surprised." He rose and began to pace. "Can't you give me a little time to process this? You've known about the baby for five months—I only found out hours ago."

Anger bubbled up in Molly's chest. "And whose fault is that?" she snapped. "I called several times, trying to find out when you'd be back so I could tell you in person."

"I know," he said weakly.

"I get that you're shocked, but don't act like I tried to keep this a secret from you."

"I know," he repeated. His shoulders rose and fell as he let out a long sigh. "And I'm sorry I didn't respond—I truly am. But are you ever going to forgive me for that? Or are you going to stay mad forever?"

His question took some of the wind out of her sails. She was forced to admit he had a point, though that didn't mean she was ready to let go of her hurt and anger quite yet. Still, if they were going to move forward, they would have to find a way to forgive each other for these misunderstandings.

It was the least their daughter deserved.

"I'm not going to continue to punish you," she said finally. "But I spent the last five months feeling used and disposable. It's going to take me a little time to get over that."

Max nodded. "I'm sorry I made you feel that way." He walked back over to the side of her bed. "If

I had known…" He shook his head. "Well, we can't change the past. So I'll make a deal with you—I'll be patient with you if you can be patient with me."

That sounded reasonable. "I can do that." It would be hard not to think the worst whenever Max didn't appear excited or interested in baby stuff, but she'd just have to remind herself he was still adjusting to the thought of fatherhood. He'd probably never imagined having a child like this. She couldn't really blame him for his reaction—she wasn't exactly thrilled about having a baby with a man who didn't even live in the same town, but like Max had said, she couldn't change the past.

His light green eyes warmed as he stared down at her. "Thanks," he said simply.

"It's only fair," she replied.

He was quiet a moment. "So," he began, "how are you feeling? Are you getting morning sickness or anything?"

Molly shook her head. "Not anymore. It was a bit rough at first, but I started feeling better a few weeks ago."

"That's good," he said. He glanced at her belly, clearly trying to think of something to say. "Can you feel it—uh, her," he corrected immediately, his cheeks turning pink. "Can you feel her move yet?"

Molly nodded, smiling as the baby shifted inside her. "She's actually moving now. Do you want to try to feel her?"

"Really?" A note of hope was plain in his tone.

"Really." Molly took his hand and placed it on her

lower belly. "Push in a little," she instructed. Max did as she said, and a few seconds later the baby kicked. "Did you feel that?"

She realized as soon as she saw his face the question had been unnecessary. Max looked both awed and surprised, his eyes shining with wonder.

"That was really strong!" He sounded delighted. His obvious excitement helped smooth the edges of Molly's hurt emotions, and she felt herself softening toward him.

"Is it always like that?" he asked.

Molly shook her head. "Not yet. It mostly feels like flutters when she moves. But my doctor told me as she gets bigger and starts to run out of room, I'll feel her movements a lot more."

"That's amazing," he said. "Does it seem strange, or are you used to it by now?"

He seemed genuinely curious, which was another point in his favor. Molly let her guard drop another inch...

"At first it was kind of weird," she confessed, smiling a bit at the memory. "I wasn't used to sharing my body like that, you know?"

He nodded, then laughed. "Actually, I don't know. But I can imagine."

"I've gotten used to it. But there are still days when I feel like she's taking over."

"When is she due?"

"September 25," she replied. "At least, that's the hope. My OB told me first babies don't always cooperate."

"Let's hope this one will."

"This one will what?"

The new voice in the room made Molly jump. Both she and Max looked at the door to find Blaine standing just inside the room. "Sorry," he said, a bit sheepishly. "I did knock."

His gaze zeroed in on Max's hand, still on her belly. Blaine's eyes narrowed as he looked at Max, then at her.

Max jerked his hand away. He was clearly flustered, but he covered it by walking over to Blaine. "Good to see you, man."

"You, too." The pair engaged in the standard male one-armed embrace/chest bump ritual. "You okay?" Blaine said, nodding at Max's sling.

"Just a little strain," he answered. "No big deal. What about you?" Max jerked his chin at the bruise darkening the side of Blaine's face.

"Yeah, I'm okay. Got tossed around a bit in the avalanche, but all's well that ends well."

Blaine turned to Molly. "What about you?" He walked over to the bed, peering at her head. "Looks like you've got a nasty bruise there."

Molly reached up to gingerly touch her forehead. In truth, she'd forgotten about the bump in the wake of the ultrasound. "I think it looks worse than it is," she said, though in truth, it would probably hurt more tomorrow.

"I'm glad you're both okay," Blaine said. "I was worried."

"So were we," Max said drily. "But the rescuers were absolute pros."

"Was anyone else hurt?" Molly asked. Since they'd been brought straight to the hospital, she hadn't gotten an up-close view of the aftermath of the avalanche. Even though it hadn't looked like there had been much property damage, it was possible skiers and snowboarders had been caught up in the wall of snow and ice.

"From what I've heard, the injuries aren't too serious," Blaine said. "Josh and Tilda are okay. Josh and I actually got caught up in it—we had quite a ride down the mountain."

"My God," Molly gasped. "That sounds terrifying."

"Oh, yeah," Blaine confirmed. "Fortunately, Josh had a transponder on his jacket, so the rescuers knew right where to find us. We're both a little bruised, but nothing bad." He clenched and unclenched his hand, wincing a bit. "Somehow I managed to keep hold of him the whole way down."

Molly smiled. "Sounds like those paternal instincts took over."

"And a good thing, too," Blaine said. "I just got him. I'm not about to lose him now."

"Is there a lot of property damage?" Max asked.

Blaine shook his head. "I don't think so. Overall, we got really lucky with this one."

"That's good," Molly said. "Is the road to The Lodge clear? Or are guests stranded up there?"

"They're stuck for now," Blaine replied. "But the

crews estimate they'll have the roads clear again by tomorrow morning."

Molly nodded. "I'll call my staff and ask them to do an extra check on the guests. Do you know if there's enough food on site to accommodate everyone?"

Blaine and Max exchanged a look. "I don't know," Blaine replied. "And I don't think you need to worry about it right now."

"I have to do my job," she protested.

Max piped up. "Or maybe you could let the people who weren't trapped on a gondola for the last six hours take care of things while you focus on resting."

"That sounds like a good idea to me," Blaine said, nodding emphatically.

Molly glanced from one man to the other. "You don't have to gang up on me," she muttered.

"Mols, everyone at work knows you were stuck on that gondola," Blaine said. "No one is expecting to hear from you right now. In fact, the world won't stop turning if you take a couple of days off."

"I don't know," she said doubtfully.

"It'll be good for you," Blaine pressed. "You might feel fine now, but a scare like the one you had can come back to bite you later. I know I'm going to take a little time off to keep an eye on Josh."

"He's right," Max confirmed.

"Besides, I'm sure the rest of the family would appreciate it if you stayed at sea level for a little bit. Where is Mason, anyway?" he asked. "I figured your brother would be here to check on you."

"He, ah, doesn't know I'm here," Molly said. "I didn't tell my family I was trapped in the gondola."

Blaine raised one eyebrow. "Why not?"

"I didn't want to worry them." It had seemed like a good idea earlier, but in the face of Blaine's scrutiny, Molly wondered if she'd made the right decision.

"I see." Blaine shrugged. "Well, the cat's out of the bag now. The media was all over the rescue effort, and it's only a matter of time until your names are released to the press. You might want to give your brother a heads-up before he hears it on the television."

"I will," Molly said. But just the thought of talking to Mason right now was exhausting. She knew her family deserved to know the details of her ordeal, but she simply wasn't up to dealing with their reactions. Maybe she could send out a reassuring text and call them in the morning, after she'd had some sleep...

"You look tired," Blaine said, not unkindly. "I'm going to step out and make a few phone calls, get this guy a place to stay. Then I'll come back, and after you're released, I'll take you home."

"I can get a cab," she protested, but Blaine shook his head.

"This isn't a debate," he said. "I'm not going to let my cousin take a cab home from the hospital."

"But I don't know when I'll be getting released," she protested. "You can't stay here all night—Joshua and Tilda need you," she said, referring to her cousin's son and girlfriend. Blaine had recently reconnected with Tilda, his high school sweetheart and the mother of the son he hadn't known he had. Molly knew they were all trying to make up for lost time, and she hated to be the reason Blaine wasn't with his family tonight.

"It's fine," he said. "They'll both understand. Who do you think sent me here after we learned you'd been in the gondola all afternoon? Tilda wants me to make sure you're okay. No more arguments," he said, just as she opened her mouth again.

Molly finally nodded, recognizing she wasn't going to win this one. "Thank you," she said quietly.

"Of course," Blaine replied. He looked at Max. "Let's get you squared away."

Some unspoken communication passed between the two men. Max nodded his head, a hint of wariness in his eyes. "Sounds good," he said. He turned to Molly. "I hope you get some rest tonight."

"Thank you." Disappointment welled up inside her chest, but she quickly quashed it. Of course Max couldn't acknowledge the nature of their connection in front of Blaine—no one knew they had been seeing each other. "Maybe I'll see you at The Lodge before your stay is over."

"I hope so," he said. She could tell by the look in his eyes he wanted to say more, but Max settled for a nod before turning and following Blaine out of the room.

Molly leaned back against the thin hospital pillow with a sigh. A few moments ago she'd been hopeful about the future. But if Max couldn't bring himself to share their relationship in front of Blaine—a fellow veteran and friend—would he ever be able to go public with the news?

She rested her hand on her belly. "We've got a long road ahead of us, little one," she whispered. "But no matter what, I will always be here for you."

Max braced himself, certain Blaine would fire at him with both barrels once they were away from Molly. But his friend merely led him down the hall to a cluster of chairs, a makeshift waiting room of sorts.

Blaine took one seat, pulling his phone from his pocket as he did. Max took a seat nearby, feeling a bit on edge.

"We need to find you a hotel, buddy," Blaine said. He tapped on his phone screen as he spoke, apparently gathering information. "There's a B and B not far from here, or you can stay at the discount motel chain for the night."

"There's really no way up the mountain tonight?"

Blaine shook his head. "I'm afraid not. Don't worry—The Lodge will comp your stay. It's the least we can do, given what happened today."

A spike of worry needled Max. "I don't mean to be a diva, but I can't stay in town. I need to get back up the mountain sooner rather than later."

"Furbert came with you?" Blaine asked, correctly guessing the reason for Max's sense of urgency.

"Yes." And although Max had been sure to leave out food and water, the dog would need to be let out before morning.

"Does he do okay with strangers? Because I can have one of our people check on him."

"That should work," Max said. He rattled off a few of the commands Furbert was used to hearing, to make it easier on the staffer who checked on him.

Blaine nodded. "No problem." His fingers flew across the screen as he typed out a message. "It's done," he said, glancing up a minute later.

"Thanks," Max said. Knowing Furbert was going to be taken care of helped ease his mind.

"Anytime," Blaine said. "So…how long have you and Molly been together?"

The question came without warning, as if it were just another topic of regular conversation between them.

Max shifted. "I don't know that we're really together," he hedged.

"I see," Blaine replied. "So how long have the two of you been hooking up?"

Max frowned. "Hooking up" was too crass a description for what they were doing. "It's more than that," he protested. What they had went beyond mere sex—Max felt intensely connected to Molly on an emotional and spiritual level, as well.

He just didn't know what to do about it.

"All right," Blaine said with exaggerated patience. "It's complicated, I get it. But you still haven't answered my question."

"Two years," Max said.

Blaine's eyes widened. "Isn't that how long you've been coming here to relax?"

Max nodded. There was something freeing about telling his buddy this secret. He knew discretion was important to Molly, but he was talking to Blaine now as a friend, not an employee of The Lodge. And given the personal nature of Blaine's question, Max felt certain he was trying to determine if his cousin was okay, not if a fellow employee was engaging in ill-advised behavior with a guest.

"Wow," Blaine said softly. "I had no idea."

"That was by design," Max replied.

The other man processed this for a few seconds. Then he said, "And now she's pregnant."

It wasn't a question. Max knew Blaine had put two and two together when he'd stepped into the hospital room. Still, Max stiffened defensively. He'd only known about the baby for a few hours—he hadn't had time to process the news properly. Talking about Molly's pregnancy wasn't something he wanted to do right now. But he couldn't ignore his friend.

"Yeah," he said with a sigh.

"I take it from your reaction this is a shock?"

Max nodded.

"How far along is she?" Blaine asked.

"About five months," Max replied.

"Whoa. That's half the pregnancy." Blaine frowned slightly. "That doesn't sound like Molly," he said, almost to himself. "I can't believe she kept something like this a secret from you for so long."

"She didn't," Max said quickly. It was important Blaine knew she had contacted him; he didn't want Molly's cousin thinking the worst of her.

Max leaned forward in his chair, glancing around to make sure they were alone. There was a man sitting on a small sofa a few feet away, but he appeared to be asleep. "She reached out to me several times over the past few months. But I was so wrapped up in a major fund-raising push I didn't get back to her."

"But now you know."

"Yeah." He leaned back with a sigh. "She blurted it out when the avalanche hit. Things were pretty dicey there for a few minutes. I think she was afraid we were going to die, so she wanted me to know."

"Man." Blaine shook his head. "That's a memorable way to find out you're going to be a father."

Max actually laughed. "Tell me about it."

"What are you going to do?"

"I'm not sure," Max admitted. "We weren't exactly planning this, you know?"

"Yes, I'm familiar with that feeling," Blaine drawled. Tilda, Blaine's high school sweetheart, had gotten pregnant on their prom night. She thought she had miscarried their baby, but when she'd realized the truth, Blaine had already left for basic training. Blaine had missed a lot of time with his son, and Max knew his friend was thrilled to have the boy in his life now.

"Two years is a long time to be together, though," Blaine continued.

Max shook his head. "It was never anything formal," he said. "More of an understanding. And I'm not quite sure what Molly expects of me now. She's not exactly demanding a ring."

"She won't," Blaine cut in. "That's not her style, and you should know that by now."

The subtle rebuke stung, but it was the truth. Molly wasn't the type of woman to beg, especially not for something as important as a serious commitment.

"Obviously, I'm going to make sure Molly and the baby are taken care of," Max said. "I'm just not sure about the rest."

Blaine studied him for a moment, his expression unreadable. "What's holding you back?"

Max shifted, his friend's scrutiny making him uncomfortable. "You know I tried the marriage thing before. It didn't work."

"Molly isn't Beth," Blaine pointed out.

It was true, but that didn't make the thought of marriage any more appealing. "I think I'm just not cut out for marriage."

"Hmm." Blaine sounded unimpressed.

"What?" Max sounded defensive, but he didn't care. It was clear the other man had something more to say. Might as well let him get it out of his system.

Blaine narrowed his eyes. "You're scared, dude. I get it. But if you think being a part-time dad is going to be a viable long-term strategy, you've got another think coming."

"I never said—" Max began, but Blaine cut him off.

"You're thinking you and Molly can carry on as before. You come for a visit once every three months, and in the meantime, you cut her some checks to make sure the kid has everything they need. I'm telling you right now, that's not going to work. Molly deserves more than that, and so does your child."

Max clenched his jaw, anger building in his chest. No one had talked to him like this before, at least not since his time in basic training. The fact that Blaine was his friend was the only thing keeping Max from unleashing his temper and giving the man a verbal beatdown.

"You done?" he said, his voice tight.

Blaine actually smiled, as if he was enjoying Max's reaction. "For now," he said. He stood, then reached down and grabbed Max's arm to pull him out of the chair. "Come on, let's get you to that B and B. More and more press are descending on the town to cover the avalanche. The motel will be crawling with them." He slapped Max's good shoulder. "You've got a lot to think about. A good night's sleep will help."

"I hope you're right," Max muttered, his anger draining away as fatigue took center stage. He *was* tired. Even though being trapped in the gondola hadn't been physically strenuous, the cold and stress of the ordeal had taken their toll on his body. Once upon a time, he'd endured far worse conditions for far longer and come out the other side fine. But his tolerance had waned since retiring from the military. Normally, he didn't notice the difference. Now, though? He felt weak and far older than his thirty-seven years.

Blaine glanced over and slowed his pace. "It's going to be okay, buddy," he said. "You don't have

Dear Reader,

**IT'S A FACT:** if you answer 4 quick questions, we'll send you 4 FREE REWARDS!

I'm not kidding you. As a leading publisher of women's fiction, we value your opinions… and your time. That's why we are prepared to **reward** you handsomely for completing our mini-survey. In fact, we have 4 Free Rewards for you, including 2 free books and 2 free gifts.

As you may have guessed, that's why our mini-survey is called **"4 for 4".** Answer 4 questions and get 4 Free Rewards. It's that simple!

Thank you for participating in our survey,

*Pam Powers*

to figure everything out tonight. You and Molly have time to decide what to do next."

"Yeah," Max said, only half-convinced. They'd already lost so much time—he didn't want to waste any more being indecisive.

"Cut yourself some slack," Blaine advised. "You've had a hell of a day. Tomorrow will be better."

"I thought the only easy day was yesterday," Max joked.

Blaine shook his head and made a face. "What, are you a SEAL now? Get out of here with that crap."

"Just trying to embrace the suck," Max said, smiling at his friend's reaction.

"That's not a bad strategy," Blaine replied. "But a word of advice? Don't say that in front of Molly. I can tell you from experience, women generally don't appreciate the poetic nature of military expressions."

They pushed open a set of double doors and walked into the parking lot. A cold wind gusted, sending small piles of snow swirling along the asphalt. Max shivered a bit, but was immediately distracted by the sight of several news trucks parked close to the hospital.

"My God," he said softly, slowing his pace to take in the line of reporters standing in the cold, huddled and shivering as they clutched microphones and spoke into cameras. "You weren't kidding. It's a zoo out here."

"Keep moving," Blaine muttered. "And don't make eye contact."

They walked faster, heads down. But they made it only a few feet before a voice shouted out, "Hey, it's the man from the gondola!"

Max swore under his breath.

"Green truck, straight ahead," Blaine directed. They jogged for it, ignoring the commotion behind them as half a dozen reporters and their attendant camera crews thundered across the parking lot in pursuit.

"Buckle up, buddy," Blaine advised as they slammed the truck doors shut. "This is gonna be fun."

Blaine gunned it. Max was slammed back in the seat as the truck shot forward, pulling out of the parking spot before the reporters had a chance to pen them in. Max glanced in the side mirror as they put the hospital behind them. The media folks had already begun to trudge back toward their original spots, close to the ER entrance.

He was glad they'd escaped the scrum, but worry washed over him as he thought about Molly. "You can't drag Molly through that," he said. Part of him wanted Blaine to turn around so Max could stay with Molly and guard her from any overly nosy reporters who might try to get into her room. But he knew their return would only heighten the media furor…

"I won't," Blaine replied, sliding him a glance before returning his focus to the road.

"Promise me," Max demanded. "She shouldn't have to run through a cold parking lot after everything she's been through today."

"I'm a highly trained operative, with loads of experience in both covert operations and hostage extractions," Blaine drawled. "I think I can sneak my cousin out of the hospital without the press getting wind of it."

"Maybe I should help," Max mused. "I could create a distraction, draw their attention."

"Or you could stay in and get some rest," the other man said. He pulled into the driveway of a large Victorian-style house. Light shone through the windows, casting golden squares on the floorboards of the wraparound porch. The place looked friendly and welcoming, but Max couldn't get his mind off Molly, alone in the hospital room.

*Well, not exactly alone*, he thought. The baby was with her.

The thought should have brought him comfort, but instead only heightened his worry. He was so wrapped up in his thoughts he didn't notice that Blaine had climbed out of the truck. Suddenly, the passenger door swung open.

"Let's go," Blaine said.

"I think I should stay and help you," Max replied. "Make sure Molly gets home okay."

"Nope." Blaine grabbed his arm and tugged him out of the truck. "You're going to head inside. They're expecting you." He reached past Max and locked the door before slamming it shut.

"Wait!" Max protested, as Blaine circled around the hood and climbed into the driver's seat once more.

Blaine rolled the window down a crack. "I'll be

back in the morning," he called. "Sleep well, princess!"

Max stood in the driveway, amusement and frustration swirling in his chest as he watched Blaine drive away. Deep down, he knew his friend would take care of Molly.

"Maybe it's for the best," he told himself as he turned and headed up the stairs to the house. Molly was probably happy to have a break from him, given the fact that they'd been trapped together all day. A little time apart might help them both. After all, they were going to be seeing each other a lot over the next few days.

But as Max stepped inside the warmth of the house, a small voice in his head wondered if he would ever get tired of being around her.

# Chapter 8

Someone was pounding on her door.

Molly groaned and rolled over in bed, squinting at the clock on her nightstand. Eight seventeen in the morning. Who could possibly be visiting now?

Normally, she was already up and about and on her way to work by this time. But she hadn't been released from the hospital until around ten thirty last night. True to his word, Blaine had returned to give her a ride home. He'd draped a jacket over her shoulders, placed a ball cap on her head and led her out a side door. "You don't want to get caught by the press," he'd said.

Molly hadn't argued. At that point, she'd been so tired she would have agreed to almost anything if it had meant getting closer to her bed. Blaine had dropped her off around eleven, but before she could go to sleep, she'd wanted to take a hot bath and wash the day off her skin.

She'd finally crawled between the sheets a little after midnight, feeling warm for the first time in hours.

Sleep had claimed her quickly, but her dreams had not been peaceful. She frowned as images flitted through her mind: Max, standing cold and unmoving as she tried to hand him their baby. Then his face twisting in cruel smile as he grabbed the baby from her arms, walking away as she lay chained to a hospital bed, unable to follow. It didn't take a psychiatrist to interpret those nightmares.

She shook her head to dismiss the disturbing thoughts. She stared at the ceiling for a few seconds, trying to muster the motivation to get up and answer the door. But her bed was so comfortable, and her head ached…

The knocking stopped. *Oh, good*, she thought, closing her eyes once more. Whoever was at her door had given up; she could go back to sleep in peace.

An electronic jingle started up from the direction of her nightstand. Molly muttered a curse as she reached out, fumbling blindly for the phone. She opened her eyes a slit, pressed the green button on the screen and closed her eyes again.

"Hello?"

"Open the damn door, Molly," her brother demanded.

She sighed heavily. "Good morning to you, too, Mason."

"I'm serious, Mols. Let us in."

"Us?" She really wasn't in the mood for company. Mason was one thing—she could handle him. But she didn't want a large audience this morning.

"Elaine is with me," he said, referring to his wife.

He wasn't going to leave her alone until she relented—she knew from experience that her brother was nothing if not stubborn. "Give me a minute," she told him, ending the call before he could reply.

She pushed herself up, swinging her legs over the side of the bed. The change in position triggered a wave of dizziness, but it passed quickly. Moving slowly, she shoved her feet into slippers and grabbed her robe.

She opened her front door to find Mason standing on the welcome mat, fist raised to start pounding again. Molly lifted one eyebrow. "Really? I told you I was coming."

"You took your time about it."

She shook her head as she turned around and trudged into the kitchen. Footsteps sounded behind her as Mason and Elaine followed.

"To what do I owe this early-morning pleasure?" she said, making a beeline for the coffee maker.

"Why didn't you tell us you were trapped on the gondola yesterday?" Mason demanded.

"I didn't want you to worry," she replied. The heavenly smell of coffee rose into the air as she scooped fresh grounds into the filter. She added water to the reservoir, then pressed the start button. *Soon*, she thought longingly.

Mason touched her shoulder. She turned to really look at her brother for the first time since his arrival. His normally styled hair was mussed, as if he'd been running his hands through it. Instead of his usual suit and tie, he was wearing torn jeans and a college sweatshirt that had seen better days. "Of course I worried," he said, pulling her in for a hug.

"We had to find out about it through the news," Elaine chided, her voice dripping with disapproval. Her long blond hair was pulled back in a messy bun and she wore only a hint of lip gloss on her otherwise bare face. Yet she still managed to look like a cover model, even in her yoga pants and slim-fitting fleece jacket.

Molly felt a niggle of insecurity about her own appearance. She hadn't bothered to comb her hair or brush her teeth before answering the door, and her comfortable pajamas and fuzzy robe left much to be desired in terms of fashion. But she wasn't planning on going out today, so really, what did it matter how she looked?

"I'm sorry," Molly said as her brother released her. "I didn't think it was going to take so long to get out of there, and I didn't want to scare anyone."

"That's what family is for," Mason pointed out. "If I had known you were up there, I could have—"

"What?" she cut in. "What exactly could you have done?" Her brother looked as if she'd slapped him, so she softened her tone. "I appreciate the thought, but we were in contact with the rescue team the whole time. There wasn't much to do but wait. I knew if I told you I was in the gondola, you would have been climbing the walls, or worse, getting in the way as you tried to 'help' the rescuers do their job. Besides, I figured you had your own job to worry about."

Mason was the director of sales for the Colton Empire, the family nickname for the all-encompassing company that included The Lodge, The Chateau and several other properties in Roaring Springs. As a popular, smooth-talking businessman, Mason had likely spent much of yesterday afternoon reassuring investors and potential clients in the wake of the avalanche.

"That still doesn't mean I had to find out from a reporter!"

"You're right, and I apologize. I didn't know it was going to be such a news spectacle. But I'm fine, so let's move on."

He eyed her forehead. "You don't look fine."

Molly touched the bump on her head with gentle fingers. "The swelling has actually gone down."

"It looks terrible," Elaine said snidely.

Instead of replying, Molly sighed and poured herself a cup of coffee. She gestured to the pot. "Help yourself."

Mason looked horrified as she raised the cup to her lips and took that first fortifying sip. "What?" she asked, frowning at him.

"Are you sure you should be drinking that in your condition?"

A chill shot through her limbs at his words. "What do you mean, my condition?" Did he know about the baby? How was that possible? She hadn't told anyone but Max and John, the man who'd lifted her to safety yesterday. She couldn't imagine either one of them had been in contact with Mason...

"There's an article in today's paper that says you're pregnant." He studied her face as he dropped this little bombshell.

"What?" Molly felt the color drain from her face. She leaned back against the counter, gripping the edge with her free hand. "Let me see."

Mason pulled out his phone, typed on the screen for a few seconds. Molly felt Elaine's eyes on her, but she couldn't meet her sister-in-law's gaze.

She wasn't ready for people to know about the baby. She'd barely told Max, and he was the father! A sense of panic gripped her, squeezing her ribs until it was hard to breathe. She'd hoped for privacy while she and Max figured out what to do next. The situation was difficult enough without adding public scrutiny to the mix.

"Here it is," Mason said. He handed his phone over, and she stared at the screen, blinking to focus on the text.

The article was a rundown of yesterday's events, detailing the rescue with a sort of breathless tone that was perhaps better suited to a tabloid than a serious newspaper. She bristled at the description of her "clinging desperately to the mountain man of a rescuer, gratitude and attraction shining in her eyes."

But the real kicker was the last paragraph:

*But perhaps more than two lives were saved today? This reporter overheard a conversation between Maxwell Hollick, charity mogul, and an unidentified man. It sounds like Ms. Gilford is in the family way. What's more? Max Hollick might be the father! What does all this mean for Mr. Hollick's charity organization, K-9 Cadets? Will a little human soon be joining the dog pack? Time will tell!*

Molly turned to face the counter, setting down her coffee and the phone before she dropped either.

"So it's true?" Mason asked quietly.

She nodded.

Behind her, she heard Elaine suck in a breath.

"Is Maxwell Hollick the father?" Mason asked.

"It doesn't matter," she muttered.

"Of course it does!" her brother exclaimed. "I read up on this guy, Mols. He's ex-Special Forces and apparently quite well-known for his charity work. How on earth did you meet him?" His tone was skeptical, as if he couldn't quite believe a man like Max would ever be interested in a woman like her.

Anger bubbled in her chest. "Like I said, it doesn't matter."

Mason ignored her warning tone. "Why don't you want to talk about him? Are you ashamed?"

Molly turned to face her brother again. "No," she said, her voice lethally quiet.

"I don't understand why you didn't tell us about this earlier." He flung out his arms and began to pace the length of her kitchen. "We're your family, Molly. We could have helped you."

"I didn't want any help," she replied.

Mason's reaction was a perfect example of why she hadn't told her family about the baby. Her brother meant well, but since her parents had retired to spend their golden years traversing the country in their state-of-the-art luxury RV, he had appointed himself "head of the family." It was a nice thought, but Molly didn't need her younger brother lecturing her about her life choices. Their sister, Sabrina, felt the same way. She'd recently graduated from college, but rather than return to Roaring Springs to settle down in a job, she'd elected to stay in Denver and live with some friends. Molly was happy for her younger sister, but according to some texts she'd received from Sabrina, Mason wanted her to come home.

"Molly—" he began, but she cut him off before he could start up again.

"Enough," she said, making a slashing gesture with her hand. "I'm not going to discuss this with you."

Mason snapped his mouth shut, a hurt look entering his blue eyes. He stared at her for a moment, as if expecting her to say or do something. But Molly simply returned his gaze, refusing to engage with him on this issue.

Sighing softly, he reached behind her to retrieve his phone from the counter. "May I use your bathroom before we go?" He sounded subdued, almost disappointed.

"Of course."

He walked away, leaving her alone with Elaine.

Molly turned to face her sister-in-law. Elaine was no stranger to the little tensions that flared up between the Gilford siblings. Still, Molly hated to argue in front of her.

"I'm sorry about that," she said, the words trailing off as she saw the look on Elaine's face.

The other woman was staring at her belly with a look of such naked yearning it broke Molly's heart. *Oh, no*, she thought, guilt washing over her like a tidal wave.

It was no secret Mason and Elaine had been trying for a baby. A few months ago, Mason had mentioned they were having trouble in that department, but he'd waved away Molly's expressions of sympathy.

"It'll happen eventually," he'd said confidently.

But given Elaine's current expression, it seemed things were still not working out the way they wanted.

Molly reached for the other woman, intent on comforting her. Elaine jerked away, her eyes flickering up to Molly's face. "Don't touch me!" she snapped.

"Elaine, I'm so sorry," Molly began.

She laughed, but there was no humor in the sound. "Is that right? Well, I guess that just makes everything better now, doesn't it?"

Not knowing what to say, Molly pivoted to pick up her coffee cup. When she glanced back, Elaine's look had turned to one of disgust.

"I don't understand," she said, shaking her head for emphasis. "Mason and I have wanted a baby for so long. I know he told you. But did you know how long we've been trying? Two years. Two years of disappointment after disappointment, with nothing to show for our efforts. Do you know how many times I've been poked and prodded? How many painful procedures I've gone through, all in an attempt to figure out why my body doesn't work the way it should?"

Molly said nothing, knowing there were no words that could offer the other woman any comfort.

"And then," Elaine continued, her voice rising in pitch and volume, "you get yourself knocked up on what amounts to little more than a glorified one-night stand! Tell me how that's fair?"

Molly inwardly cringed at her sister-in-law's description of events, but didn't respond.

"You don't even want this baby, do you?" Elaine threw the question out like a gauntlet, a challenge of sorts that Molly knew she couldn't win.

"That's not true." But even as she uttered the words, a memory flashed in her mind. Seeing those two lines pop up on the pregnancy test had filled her with doubt and worry, and for a time, Molly had vacillated between her options. Shock and stress had kept her from feeling like a mother, made her question if she even wanted to be one at this time in her life.

Things had changed during her first OB appointment. They'd performed an ultrasound to make sure everything looked okay so far, and Molly had seen the baby for the first time. She hadn't been much to look at then—she'd had the appearance of a small gray gummy bear. But the instant Molly had seen the image, a fierce love had filled her, smothering all her doubts and worries.

Now? She couldn't wait to meet her daughter, to hold her for the first time and kiss her petal-soft cheeks. Just the thought of it warmed her from the inside and made her want to smile.

Elaine ignored her protest. "Oh, please." She grabbed a paper towel from the roll on the counter and dabbed her eyes. Molly ached to hug her, but knew the other woman wouldn't welcome the gesture.

"And the worst part?" Her sister-in-law wrapped her arms around herself, shaking a little as she did. "Mason would make such a wonderful father. Your baby daddy probably can't even be bothered to return your calls."

That barb hit a little too close to home. Tears pricked Molly's eyes. "I didn't do this to hurt you," she said. "I love you and Mason too much to ever deliberately cause you pain."

Elaine met her gaze, her green eyes wide and red-rimmed. "That should have been my baby," she sniffed. "Not yours."

Frustration welled in Molly's chest, testing the limits of her sympathy. "My pregnancy has no bearing on your ability to have a baby. It's not like there are only a finite amount of babies to go around—you and Mason can still get pregnant."

"No, we can't," she said flatly. "We've exhausted all of our options. The fertility treatments didn't work, and we can't afford to keep trying."

The revelation shocked Molly into silence for a few seconds. "I'm so sorry," she said finally. "I had no idea."

Elaine didn't say anything—she simply stared into space. Molly wasn't certain the other woman had even heard her.

The silence in the kitchen was broken by Mason's return. He half stumbled into the room, clutching his phone in one hand. His expression was a combination of shock and disbelief, and his face was so pale Molly instinctively reached for him, fearing he might fall down.

"What is it?" she asked. Her heart started to pound—something was clearly wrong with her brother.

He shook his head, as if trying to fling off a net. "The avalanche," he said. "It's uncovered the bodies of several women."

"Oh, no," Molly cried. "That's terrible." She frowned, confused. "But I thought the rescuers said yesterday there weren't any fatalities?"

"These are…old bodies," Mason said, grimacing. "Victims."

Molly shook her head. It was unsettling news to be sure, but why was Mason so distraught?

"There's more, isn't there?" A stone of worry

formed in her stomach as apprehension sent a chill down her spine.

Mason nodded, his eyes shiny with unshed tears. "Sabrina," he whispered.

Their sister's name sent a jolt through Molly. Denial welled up even as the logical part of her brain acknowledged the truth. "No." She shook her head, taking a step back. "No, no, no."

Mason rubbed his eyes with one hand, his voice muted when he spoke again.

"One of the bodies is hers. She's dead."

Furbert bounded down the trail looking like his joints were made of springs as he darted from one tree to another, stopping here to sniff, there to mark his territory. Max ambled along behind him, happy to let the dog burn off the excess energy he'd acquired from being cooped up inside yesterday afternoon and last night.

The B and B had been a nice place to stay, all things considered. Max had taken a hot shower and climbed into the too-soft bed, falling asleep almost as soon as his head had hit the pillow. It was a skill he'd retained from his soldiering days—even though his mind was occupied with a million different thoughts and worries, his body was trained to sleep whenever it got the opportunity.

He'd woken a few hours ago, his brain immediately starting up the soundtrack of questions and what-ifs that had plagued him since yesterday's revelations. But before he could indulge in some heavy-duty thinking, he'd first needed to make sure Furbert was okay.

Fortunately, Blaine's predictions had been correct. The road up the mountain had been clear, and the cab hadn't had any trouble taking him to The Lodge. Furbert had been excited to see him, practically dancing in place as Max had entered the cabin. Max had been pleased to find that fresh water and food had been set out for the dog, and furthermore, Furbert hadn't had any accidents on the carpet. Not wanting to tempt fate, Max had taken the dog for a walk before even bothering to change his clothes.

Now, as he breathed in the fresh, cool air and felt the pleasant burn of exercise in his legs, Max's head began to clear.

He was going to be a father.

A weight settled over him once again as he recalled the image on the sonogram screen: a tiny baby, arms and legs and hands and feet all immediately recognizable. The curve of chin and nose, the slope of the belly and roundness of the head; all parts there. All perfectly formed.

Real.

And part of him.

He knew that, too, without a doubt. Even if Molly had been with other men in the times they'd been apart, it didn't make sense for her to try to pin this pregnancy on him if he wasn't the real father. He was wealthy, yes, but he knew she had a trust fund so money wasn't an issue for her. Given their geographic separation, she'd be better off claiming a local man as the father rather than him. As much as he was stunned by the existence of this baby, he couldn't deny it was his.

So what should his next move be? And moreover, what did Molly expect of him?

Marriage was off the table. After his relationship with Beth had fallen apart, Max had come to the realization that he wasn't cut out for being a husband. It wasn't in his nature to be fully committed to more than one thing at once. He was so wrapped up in his work with K-9 Cadets, he simply didn't have the time or the energy to expend on a full-blown relationship.

But…he couldn't leave Molly to raise their daughter alone. He wanted to be a part of the baby's life; wanted to know her and have her know him in return. He wasn't going to be one of those deadbeat dads who only saw their kid once or twice a year, if at all. He'd had a good relationship with his own father, and wanted the same for his child, as well.

So how was he going to reconcile the demands of his work with the responsibilities of being a dad? Moreover, where did he and Molly go from here? Did they have a future together as a couple, or were they destined to remain connected only by virtue of their child? It was the million-dollar question, the one he had to find an answer for before this visit was over.

A rabbit streaked across the path, flushed from the undergrowth by Furbert's inquisitive explorations. The dog let out a happy yip and shot after the small creature, plunging headlong into the bushes.

"Furbert!" The last thing Max needed was to lose

sight of his dog on the mountain. He wasn't familiar enough with the terrain to feel comfortable letting Furbert run loose, even if the dog was having the time of his life.

A niggle of worry tickled the base of Max's spine as the seconds ticked by with no sign of the canine. Then he heard the bushes shake and let out a sigh of relief. The months of obedience training had been worth it—Furbert trotted back onto the trail, his demeanor nonchalant despite the fact that he was coated in mud from his belly down.

"Really, buddy?" Max asked with a sigh. Time to head back to the cabin so they could both get cleaned up.

Furbert put up a token protest at the sight of the bathtub, but Max was able to coax him in with a little effort. After his own shower, Max flipped on the television, wanting some background noise as he dressed.

An attractive woman was on the screen, talking about the avalanche. "—gruesome discovery," she was saying. "So far, several bodies have been recovered, and authorities say there could be more."

Max stopped in front of the television, his attention captured. What was she talking about? Blaine had said there were no fatalities from yesterday's scare. Had he been misinformed?

"How long have the bodies been hidden?" asked a news anchor from off-screen.

The woman frowned into the camera. "That's just it, Clark. Authorities are telling me some of the bodies look like they've been buried for years, while others seem to have been placed more recently." She held her hand up to her ear, listening for a few seconds. "Clark, I can now confirm that the identity of one of the bodies is that of Sabrina Gilford, a young local woman who recently graduated from college."

"Was she ever reported missing?" asked the anchor.

"No," replied the woman. "Our sources say she was not listed as a missing person."

The news anchor and reporter continued their back-and-forth, but Max couldn't hear them over the rush of blood in his ears.

Sabrina Gilford. Molly's sister.

Did she already know her sister's body had been found? God, he hoped so. The thought that she had learned about her sister's death from a news report made him simultaneously heartsick and angry.

He threw on some clothes, a sense of urgency pushing him forward. He had to get to Molly, had to know if she was okay. She must be devastated—he couldn't let her suffer alone.

"Let's go," he called to Furbert as he shoved his feet into shoes. After yesterday's accident, he wasn't leaving the dog alone in the cabin any longer than necessary. But beyond that, he wasn't certain if Molly would allow him to comfort her. If she wanted nothing to do with him, she might at least respond to Furbert...

He clipped the leash onto the dog's collar, then set off quickly down the path for the main lodge. Keeping one eye on the ground, he thumbed through the contacts on his phone until he pulled up Blaine's number.

"Yeah?" Max could tell by the tone of his friend's voice he had heard the news.

"Can you take me to Molly?"

"I spoke to her earlier this morning. She doesn't want company."

"Please," Max said, dodging a low-hanging branch. "I won't bother her. I just want to bring Furbert for her."

Blaine sighed heavily. "Okay. But promise me you won't try to argue if she wants you to leave."

"Of course I won't," Max said. "I'll be in the main lobby in a few minutes."

"Roger that."

Max shoved the phone into his pocket and picked up the pace. *Hang on, Molly*, he thought. *I'm coming.*

# Chapter 9

Someone was at her door again.

Molly sat on the couch, feeling numb as she heard the knocks. It wasn't Mason, that much she knew. He and Elaine had left shortly after hearing the news of Sabrina's death. Molly would have liked for him to stay so they could comfort each other, but she didn't feel right around Elaine at the moment. It was going to take time for the memories of her sister-in-law's tirade to fade and for her hurt feelings to recover.

Normally, Molly would talk to Mason about what his wife had said, but she wasn't about to pile more on him at the moment. She'd seen them to the door, then settled on the sofa and tried to process what was happening between fielding phone calls from concerned and shocked relatives.

As the knocking persisted, Molly considered going back to bed and drawing the covers over her head. Maybe if she went back to sleep, she'd wake later to find this was all a nightmare conjured by stress. Surely her sister wasn't really dead! Molly had heard from her not that long ago—Sabrina had been headed out to a bar with friends. Her sister had seemed normal, with no indication that there was anything bothering her. How, then, had she ended up buried in the snow in Roaring Springs?

*It's a mistake*, Molly decided. That had to be it. The body recovered probably looked like Sabrina, but it wasn't really her.

She got to her feet. Might as well answer the door, tell whoever was on the other side that her sister was fine. Then she'd call Mason—he'd be so happy to know it was all just a misunderstanding.

Max and Furbert stood on the porch, both sporting worried expressions.

Molly blinked in surprise. "Uh, how did you get here?"

"Blaine brought us," Max said. He turned and waved.

Looking past his shoulder, she saw Blaine in his truck. He rolled down the window. "I know you didn't want to be bothered, but I thought you might like to see the dog," her cousin yelled.

Molly glanced down at Furbert, who was staring up at her with kind eyes. The muscles of her throat tightened, making it hard for her to speak. So she nodded instead.

"Call me when you want me to take 'em back," Blaine continued. He stared at her with such open concern that she nearly started crying on the spot. But that was silly, when she knew everything was okay.

"Thanks," she managed to choke out. "I will."

She stepped back to allow Max and Furbert inside her home. Max stopped in the hallway, waiting for her to shut the door. When she turned back, she found him watching her with his brow furrowed.

"Where's your sling?" She gestured to his arm, no longer held in place against his chest.

"What? Oh, I took it off. I'm fine," he said dismissively.

Molly shrugged, accepting his assessment.

"How are you?" he asked quietly. He grimaced. "I know that's a ridiculous question, under the circumstances, but I don't know what else to say."

"I'm okay," she replied. Surprise flickered across his face. "No, really, I am." She began to walk toward the den, dog and man following her.

She reached for her phone and sat on the couch. "It's a mistake, you see," she said, pulling up her list of contacts. "I was just getting ready to call Sabrina when you knocked on the door."

Max stood in front of her, his green eyes full of sympathy as she dialed. The phone rang and rang, until finally, her sister's voice mail picked up.

Hmm. That was strange. Normally Sabrina answered when she called her.

"It's me," Molly said. "Call me when you get this, please."

She hung up, shot Max a glance. "She's probably busy."

"Molly," he murmured softly. He knelt in front of her, reached for her hands.

"I know," she said, lifting them up so he couldn't touch her. "I'll text her. Maybe she's in a movie or something and can't answer her phone." She typed out a quick message, then leaned back and waited for her sister's response.

Max said nothing. Furbert jumped onto the sofa and curled up next to her, his body a warm weight against her side and the outside of her thigh.

As the minutes ticked by with no response, Molly began to worry.

"Maybe her battery died," she said, a sick feeling spreading over her. "Or maybe her phone was stolen. Or she left it at home."

Max reached up and brushed a strand of hair behind her ear.

"She's not dead." She tried to sound forceful, but her voice shook. "She can't be."

"What did the police say?"

"I don't know. I didn't talk to them—Mason is the one who got the call." And he hadn't told her exactly what they'd said, just that Sabrina's body had been found. Molly had been so shocked at the news, she hadn't thought to question him, to find out why the police thought the body they'd found belonged to their sister.

"I'm sure he got it wrong," she insisted, tapping on her phone again. She'd simply call the police and ask for an explanation. That was probably the fastest way to get this all cleared up.

Molly was patched through to Deputy Sheriff Daria Bloom. "Ms. Gilford... I'm so sorry for your loss. How may I help you?"

"That's just it, Deputy Sheriff Bloom. I'm calling because I think there's been a mistake. My sister is in Denver—there's no way you uncovered her body today."

The line was silent for a moment. When the other woman spoke again, it was with the careful tone one used when talking to a scared child. "Ms. Gilford, I know the news must have come as a shock. But I can assure you—"

"How do you know it was Sabrina?" Molly interrupted, tired of this game.

"Several physical characteristics matched those of your sister."

"Sabrina isn't the only woman with long curly hair," Molly replied.

"Yes, ma'am," Deputy Sheriff Bloom said. Her tone was kind—she seemed like a nice woman, but Molly wasn't in the mood for placations. "However, there were other identifying marks we used to make the identification."

"I want to see the body," Molly declared. It was clear she wasn't getting her point across over the phone. She simply needed to talk to Deputy Sheriff Bloom in person and show her why she was wrong.

Max sucked in a breath. "Molly, no," he whispered.

"I'm not sure that's a good idea," Deputy Sheriff Bloom began, but Molly cut her off again.

"I'm going to the hospital," Molly told her. "The news said the bodies had been taken there for an initial examination. Please meet me?"

The other woman sighed. "All right, Ms. Gilford. In my experience, it's best if you don't do this alone. Is there someone who can come with you? A friend who can meet you there, perhaps?"

Molly glanced at Max. "Yes," she said, hoping he'd agree to accompany her.

"Very well," said the Deputy Sheriff. "I'll see you in an hour."

"Thank you," Molly said sincerely. In sixty minutes, this would all be cleared up.

She hung up and met Max's worried gaze. "She's going to meet me at the hospital morgue. Will you come with me?"

"You know I will," he said quietly. "But do you really think this is the best idea? Once you see her body…" He trailed off, considering his words. "There are some things you can't unsee, Molly. I don't want you to remember your sister lying on a slab in the morgue."

"I have to know," she said. "I can't accept that she's gone, not without seeing for myself."

He studied her for a moment, his green eyes so intense she felt like he was trying to see into her soul. *Let him look*, she decided. She had nothing to hide.

Finally, he nodded. "All right. I can understand that."

"Do you think…" She stopped talking as she realized the question was probably too silly to bother asking.

"Do I think what?" Max prompted in a low, gentle tone.

She took a deep breath, accepting the fact that she was about to look ridiculous. "Do you think we can bring Furbert, too?" Seeing a dead body wasn't going to be pleasant. It would be nice to have the dog around to help take her mind off things when it was all over.

"He probably can't come into the hospital with us, but he won't mind waiting in the car."

Molly nodded. "Let's bring him, then. I'll go get my keys."

*This is a bad idea.*

Max walked next to Molly through the hospital parking lot, toward the main entrance of the building. Furbert was happy to stay in the car, and he'd made sure the windows were cracked so the air didn't get too stuffy. It was still cold enough that the car wouldn't overheat—in fact, Molly had thrown a few blankets into the back seat so the dog could burrow in if he got too cold.

Confident that his dog was cared for, Max was free to totally focus on Molly. Her reaction to her sister's death bothered him. Denial was a common response to traumatic news, but she seemed to be taking it a bit far. The problem was, he didn't know what to do about it. If he tried to force her to acknowledge the truth it would only hurt her. But he couldn't stand by and watch her completely detach from reality.

Max hated for her to view her sister's body—he'd seen his share of corpses while serving overseas, and it was a sight he'd never forgotten. He didn't want Molly to have that image in her head for the rest of her life. But if that was what it was going to take for her to accept the fact that her sister was gone… Well, all he could do was support her as much as she would let him. Hopefully that would be enough.

Molly had been silent during the drive, and he hadn't pressed her to speak. There was a fragility about her, a sense that she was holding herself together through sheer force of will. He admired her strength, but at the same time, he wanted to take her in his arms and pull her close. He didn't know the right words for this situation, but he could show her with his body that she wasn't alone.

But that would have to wait. They walked through the sliding glass doors into the hospital. An information desk was situated straight ahead. By unspoken agreement, they both headed for it. Just as they reached the counter, a woman walked up. She was carrying a folder close to her chest, but behind the file Max saw a gleam from the badge she wore on a chain around her neck.

"Ms. Gilford?"

At Molly's nod, the woman held out her hand. "Deputy Sheriff Bloom."

Molly shook her hand, then Max introduced himself. "Thank you for meeting me," Molly said.

"Of course." Deputy Sheriff Bloom gestured for them to walk with her. "Before we go to the morgue, do you mind if we talk for a few minutes? There's a small office just down this hall we can use."

"Okay." Molly bit her lip. Max could tell she wasn't crazy about the delay. One of the things he admired most about Molly was her determination— if she made up her mind to do something, she was going to see it through. That was why he'd agreed to accompany her here—he'd known she was going to come, one way or another. Better for her to have a friendly face present than to do this alone.

Just as she'd said, Deputy Sheriff Bloom led them into a small room. It held a round table with a few chairs scattered around it, but not much else.

Deputy Sheriff Bloom took a seat, and Max and Molly did the same. She placed the folder on the table in front of her.

"I understand you have some questions about the process we used to identify the body of your sister." Her tone was no-nonsense, bordering on brusque. "I wanted to show you the evidence we have before you go downstairs."

Molly swallowed hard, nodding. A candle of hope flickered to life in Max's chest. If the deputy sheriff was doing what he thought she was, they might be able to convince Molly the police had gotten it right without ever visiting the morgue.

Deputy Sheriff Bloom opened the folder. "The first thing to note is that the body matches the overall physical characteristics of your sister. Her height, weight, approximate age. Her hair." She slid a photograph across the table, and Max spied a tangle of brown curls, stretched out on a metal table alongside a ruler.

"The next thing we look for are scars or other identifying markers." She slid another photo toward Molly, this one a picture of a tattoo. "We know from her social media accounts that your sister got a tattoo about six months ago." Another photo joined the first; Sabrina grinning as she pointed to an identical tattoo on her arm.

Molly's face turned pale. Max felt his heart crack for her. "How did you know to look at her social media?" she whispered. "What made you think to do that in the first place?"

Deputy Sheriff Bloom's golden-brown eyes were kind as she looked at Molly. "We found her driver's license in her pocket." Another photo was slid across the table, proving the veracity of her words.

Molly let out a small moan at the sight. She reached out blindly, gripping Max's arm. He scooted closer, leaning against her so she could feel his reassuring presence.

"But we got the final confirmation this morning," Deputy Sheriff Bloom continued. "Just before we called your brother, the lab informed us the fingerprints of the body we found match those of your sister."

Molly's hand tightened around arm. "I see." She exhaled with a shudder, her body seeming to deflate into the chair.

Deputy Sheriff Bloom was quiet for a moment. When she spoke again, her voice was quiet, as if she were trying not to disturb Molly. "Would you still like to go to the morgue?"

"No." She shook her head. "No, that won't be necessary."

Molly leaned against him, her head down as she stared at her hands. Max looked at Deputy Sheriff Bloom, who was watching Molly with sympathy in her eyes.

*Thank you*, he mouthed. He draped his arm around Molly's shoulders, drawing her as close as their two chairs would allow.

Deputy Sheriff Bloom nodded in understanding. "Do you feel up to answering a few questions, Ms. Gilford? We're trying to piece together your sister's movements over the last few weeks, in the hopes of discovering when she met her killer."

It was on the tip of Max's tongue to ask if this could wait, but Molly straightened up and nodded. "I'm not sure how much help I'll be, but I'll try my best."

"Thank you." Deputy Sheriff Bloom gathered up the photographs and placed them back into her folder.

"How long…" Molly trailed off, then cleared her throat. "When did Sabrina die?"

"We're not certain yet. Once we do a cursory exam of all the victims, we're going to send them to the state facility in Denver for further testing. Based on our initial findings, though, we estimate she was killed about three weeks ago."

Molly absorbed this information with a small nod. She closed her eyes and took a deep breath. "Did she suffer?"

Max stiffened and shot a quick look at the deputy sheriff. No matter how her sister had died, there was only one answer Molly needed to hear right now.

"We think it was over quickly."

Molly let out a sigh, her shoulders relaxing a bit. She shook herself. "I'm sorry. You said you had questions for me, but I'm the one who's been doing all the asking."

"Don't apologize. You've had a terrible shock. It's only natural you want to know more about what happened."

Molly dabbed at her eyes, nodding. "I'll help you in any way I can."

"I appreciate it." Deputy Sheriff Bloom folded her hands on the table, leaning forward slightly. "Can you tell me about the last time you heard from your sister?"

"It was about a month ago," Molly said slowly. "She texted me. Said she was going out with friends."

"Did she seem normal?"

"As far as I could tell." She reached for her bag, dug out her phone. "Here are her messages." She tapped the screen, then slid the device across the table.

Max studied Molly's face as Deputy Sheriff Bloom scrolled through the messages. The color was coming back to her skin, though her eyes had a haunted look about them that he thought might linger for a while. She was clearly trying to put on a brave face, even though this had to be the worst day of her life. Her courage reminded him of the men and women he'd served with, and a surge of emotions welled in his chest; pride in her strength, sympathy for her loss, worry for how she would cope in the long term. More than all that, though, was the desire to stand by her side as she moved forward.

His thoughts were interrupted by Deputy Sheriff Bloom passing the phone back to Molly. "Thank you for that," she said. "Do you know if your sister had any enemies, anyone who might wish her harm?"

Molly frowned. "That sounds sinister."

"I don't mean to sound like she was living in a James Bond movie," Deputy Sheriff Bloom said. "But maybe she had a nasty breakup? Or a coworker she butted heads with?"

Molly shook her head. "Not that I know of…she never mentioned anything like that."

Deputy Sheriff Bloom nodded, as if she'd expected that answer. "If you remember anything she said, even in passing, please don't hesitate to reach out." She withdrew a card from her pocket and handed it to Molly. Then she stood, indicating she was done with her questions.

Max helped Molly to her feet. She stayed close to him, so he put his arm around her again. "Thanks for meeting with me," Molly said. Twin spots of color appeared on her cheeks and she ducked her head. "I know I was being unreasonable earlier. Thank you for being so kind to me."

The other woman stepped close and took one of Molly's hands between her own. "Like I said before, you don't need to apologize. I'll keep you up to date on the investigation."

"Thank you," Molly said.

The deputy sheriff nodded and walked out of the room, leaving Molly and Max alone.

"How are you doing?" he asked quietly.

She sighed, her shoulders sagging under his arm. "I'm not sure."

Taking a chance, Max kept his arm around her and pivoted to bring them face-to-face. He brought his other arm up and slowly drew her forward, giving her time to reject his embrace.

She dropped her head against his chest, sinking into the hug. Max buried his nose in her hair. "I'm so sorry, sweetheart," he said, moving one hand up and down the valley of her spine. "I wish I could make this better for you."

His heart broke as she began to cry. Quiet sniffs at first, but soon she was sobbing, her body heaving as she fought to draw in choked breaths.

Max held her close, his body absorbing her shudders as his shirt soaked up her tears. He wasn't sure how long they stood there, but gradually her breathing began to even out and the sniffles subsided.

"What can I do for you?" He wanted to help her, to charge into the fray for her, to do whatever it took to make her smile again.

"Just take me home." Her voice was dull, like a black-and-white sketch of her normal full-color self.

"All right." He took her arm and led her out of the hospital. When they neared the car, she dug into her purse and handed him the keys. "Do you remember how to get to my house?"

Max nodded, taking the keys from her hand. Without saying another word, she crawled into the back seat and reached for Furbert.

Max settled behind the wheel, eyeing the pair of them in the rearview mirror. Furbert half sat, half stood in her lap, his head leaning into her shoulder as Molly wrapped her arms around him.

"Good boy," Max murmured. He started the car and began the drive back to Molly's, one eye on the road and the other on the duo he cared for more than anything else in the world.

# Chapter 10

Molly moved on autopilot, walking from the car into her house with no true awareness of her actions. She sat on the sofa, feeling numb from the neck down. Everything was muted—the brightly colored throw pillows next to her looked pale, and sounds seemed distorted, as if she were hearing them underwater. She felt a warmth at her side; *Furbert*, she realized dimly. *I should pet him*, she thought. But she couldn't seem to muster the energy to do so.

Suddenly, Max was in front of her. He took her hands, cupped them around something warm. *Tea*.

She stared at the mug for a moment, trying to remember what to do with it. The world seemed foreign, as if she'd been dropped in a parallel universe where everything was just a bit *wrong*, a knockoff that upon closer inspection revealed itself to be a cheap imitation of the real thing.

"Molly."

The sound of her name brushed aside some of her mental fog. Max was sitting on her other side, one arm draped across the back of the sofa, his free hand helping steady the mug in her lap.

"Are you hungry?"

She blinked at the question. What did that even mean?

"She's gone."

Max's features softened. "I know."

"Why did this happen?"

He took the cup from her hands, set it on the low table in front of them. Molly missed its warmth, but she didn't bother to protest.

"I don't know."

She stared at the table until it grew blurry. "What am I supposed to do now?"

Max pulled her against his side. He was solid. Warm. Strong.

"You live," he said simply. "You remember her, try to honor her memory. You carry on."

His words made a strange kind of sense. But even though he hadn't said much, his advice seemed like an impossible task.

"I—I don't know if I can do that."

He stroked his hand up and down her arm. She focused on the sensation of his touch, an anchor in these unfamiliar waters.

"You can," he said. His voice was low and deep,

his chest rumbling against her side. "Right now, the grief is so strong you don't think you'll ever be able to function again. But little by little, you'll find a way to keep going. Your sadness won't ever leave. But you will get better at dealing with it."

She wanted to believe him, she truly did. But it sounded too good to be true. "How do you know?"

"I've lost people, too," he confided. "The circumstances were different, but they're gone all the same."

"I'm sorry," she said. Her pain was so great, she wouldn't wish this on her worst enemy.

His hand stilled on her arm. Then he chuckled softly. "You are amazing," he said.

"What do you mean?" That seemed like an odd thing to say, under the circumstances.

He pressed a kiss to the top of her head, then rested his cheek there. "You're in the middle of processing the shock of your life. And yet you're still worried about my experiences from years ago."

"If what you said is true, then the loss still hurts."

"It does," he confirmed. "But the rest of what I said is true, too. The pain isn't so acute now—it's more like a dull ache. A sore spot in my heart that I've gotten used to living with."

Maybe he was right. Maybe someday the pain would fade. But in this moment, Molly couldn't imagine a day when she wouldn't feel like her heart was being torn in two.

"She was so beautiful," she choked out. Memories of Sabrina filled her head, a movie reel of growing up together.

"Tell me about her," Max said softly. "If it doesn't hurt too much to talk about her."

"No… I think I'd like that." If she shared her memories of Sabrina, someone else would know about her. Part of her sister would still live on, in some small way.

She started talking, haltingly at first, then picking up speed as the words flowed out of her. Despite their seven-year age difference, she and Sabrina had often ganged up to pick on Mason when they were all kids. Max laughed as she recounted some of their antics, such as the time they'd woken up early one Christmas morning and hidden all of Mason's presents, convincing him that Santa had skipped him that year. Or when they'd switched the labels on some of his toiletries, so he'd reached for his mousse and wound up using shaving cream in his hair instead.

"Poor guy," Max said, his chest vibrating with laughter. "He didn't stand a chance against you two."

"Don't feel too sorry for him," Molly retorted. "He paid us back, I can assure you."

"It sounds like you were all close, despite the pranks. I'm sure your parents were happy about that."

"They were." Molly smiled, enjoying the moment of reverie. Then a black wave washed over her, stealing her breath. "Oh, my God," she said, fresh tears forming. "My parents. I have to tell them she's gone."

Furbert pressed himself against her side, apparently sensing her renewed distress. She ran one hand through his fur, grateful for the small tactile distraction. "How am I going to do this?" As bad as her pain was, she knew her parents' grief would be even more palpable. Molly hadn't even met her daughter yet, but already the thought of losing her was enough to take her breath away. How would her poor mother handle this news?

"The police may have already contacted them," Max pointed out. "If they haven't, why don't you let the deputy sheriff handle it?"

"No." Molly shook her head. As hard as it was going to be to tell them Sabrina was gone, her parents deserved to hear it from a family member. "I don't want a stranger to tell them she's dead."

"Fair enough," Max said. "But why don't you and Mason tell them together? That way, you don't have to do this alone."

She nodded. The idea of Mason helping her brought a small measure of relief. If they spoke to her parents together, her mom and dad might take comfort in knowing their two remaining children were fine, under the circumstances.

She glanced around. Where was her phone? Might as well get this over with—the news would not improve with keeping.

"Stay here," Max said. "I'll get your bag."

He rose from the couch. She felt his loss immediately, an unmooring sensation that made her stomach churn. Her hand tightened in Furbert's coat; in response, the dog shifted so that his front legs were stretched out in her lap. He pressed his head to her chest, hugging her as best as he was able.

Max returned a few seconds later. "Good boy,"

he said softly, placing her bag on the cushion he'd just left.

"He is," Molly concurred. "You know, I don't even like dogs. I don't dislike them, but I've never considered myself a dog person."

"That's okay," Max said. "Furbert won't hold it against you."

She smiled, then pulled her phone free. Keeping one hand on Furbert, she called her brother.

"Yes?" Mason sounded exhausted, as though it had taken all his energy to answer her call.

"How are you?" It was such a prosaic question, but she didn't know what else to say.

"How do you think?"

Molly immediately understood his reply. "I know," she said softly.

"It just doesn't make sense," he said, a bit of emotion seeping into his voice. "I keep going over and over it in my head, but I can't understand why she's gone."

"I know." She let him rage, listened as he said what she'd been thinking all day.

"I don't know what to do," he said finally.

"I don't, either," Molly admitted. "But I do know we need to call Mom and Dad."

Mason sighed heavily. "I…I don't think I can do that, Mols."

Molly closed her eyes, feeling a weight descend on her shoulders. "I won't make you," she said. "But it would mean a lot if you helped me do this."

"I can't." There were tears in his voice now. "I can't hurt Mom like that."

*And you think I want to?* A flush of anger rushed through her, making her want to scream. Instead, she took a deep breath. "Please, Mason. I want them to hear both our voices."

"I'm sorry, Molly. I just don't have it in me right now."

She bit her tongue, choked back the words she wanted desperately to say. Deep down inside, she recognized that adding to Mason's pain wouldn't lessen her own. "All right," she said finally. "I'll check in with you later."

"I love you." There was relief and regret in his voice, as if he knew he'd let her down but was incapable of doing anything about it.

"I love you, too." Molly ended the call and dropped her forehead to rest on Furbert.

"Come on," Max said gently. "Why don't you lie down for a bit? Collect yourself before you call them."

It was a tempting suggestion, but she knew if she didn't tell her parents now, she'd lose her nerve.

"Not yet," she replied. "I have to tell them now. It's been too long already."

"Okay."

Molly stared at Max, feeling as though she were truly seeing him for the first time that day. He'd been unquestioningly supportive, a rock she'd clung to as her emotions had raged and grief had battered her from all sides.

She'd known he was a good man—had known it from the start. But his actions today had shown her he cared about her, more than any words ever could.

Molly didn't know what their future might hold. Truly, she couldn't worry about it now, not with her sister's death still so fresh. But the mountain of anxiety she'd been carrying around ever since learning she was pregnant began to lighten.

He didn't think of her as just a fling—someone to have fun with and leave when things got too heavy. If it were that simple, he'd have left after learning about the baby. But he was here, standing beside her while she dealt with the aftermath of Sabrina's murder.

Maybe things would work out between them after all. Maybe she didn't need to be so worried about how they were going to handle adding a baby to their lives. She clung to the small hope, the only bright light in this otherwise dark time.

"Molly?"

She shook her head, dispelling the distracting thoughts. It felt wrong to even think about planning her future when Sabrina no longer had one.

"Are you sure you want to do this right now?"

*No.*

She nodded. "Yes," she said, swiping tears from her eyes. "Will you…will you stay with me?"

Max's green eyes warmed with an emotion she couldn't name. He moved her bag, then sat next to her once more.

"You know I will."

* * *

It was his stomach that woke him.

Max opened his eyes, peering into the dimly lit room. *Where am I?*

He took a deep breath. As Molly's scent filled his nose, it all clicked into place.

Molly's house. Her bedroom. Sabrina's murder.

He turned his head to the side. Sure enough, Molly was curled against him, her body warm and soft. She slept peacefully now, though she hadn't started out that way.

The call to her parents had been tough. Max had heard her mother's cries, even though Molly had kept the phone pressed to her ear. She'd sat silently, absorbing their reaction. When their screams had stopped, she'd tried to offer words of comfort through her own tears.

The whole thing had been heartbreaking. Max had felt powerless, unable to do anything but bear silent witness to Molly's agonizing pain.

When it was over, Molly had crumpled, sagging into herself like a deflating balloon. Max had scooped her up into his arms and carried her to bed. He'd intended to leave her, to let her rest while he took care of a few things he'd noticed around the house, like the trash that needed to be taken out and the dry dishes that needed to be put away. But as he'd tried to draw back, Molly gripped his wrist.

"You said you'd stay," she'd whimpered.

"If that's what you want."

At her nod, he'd slid into bed beside her. She'd

immediately embraced him, resting her head on his shoulder. Furbert had jumped onto the mattress as well, arranging himself at Molly's feet. The two of them had done their best to comfort her as she'd cried herself to sleep.

At some point, he'd fallen asleep, as well. But now he was hungry, and he was willing to bet Furbert was, too.

He glanced at his watch—just after 6:00 p.m. Time to get up and see about fixing dinner. Molly might not be interested in food, but it was important she ate something. She needed to keep up her strength for the baby.

Moving carefully, Max climbed out of bed. He took his pillow and placed it next to Molly, hoping she wouldn't miss him right away.

Furbert lifted his head in inquiry. "Stay," Max commanded softly. He didn't want Molly to be alone when she woke.

After a quick stop in the bathroom, he made it to the kitchen. A check of the freezer revealed a frozen lasagna—that would work for the two of them, but he had to find something for Furbert, as well.

He had more luck with the fridge. There was a package of ground turkey, and he found a box of rice in her pantry. "Looks like we all get to eat tonight," he muttered to himself as he began heating the oven, boiling a pot of water and cooking the meat.

Molly shambled in about twenty minutes later, Furbert at her side. She took one look at him standing by the stove and nodded. "It wasn't a dream." Her tone was matter-of-fact, with no hint of emotion.

Max shook his head. "I'm afraid not."

She didn't reply. Instead, she walked over to a cabinet, retrieved a bowl and filled it with water. She set it on the floor in the corner, then moved to the small table by the window and sat.

It was a small gesture, one that hadn't taken much effort. But the fact that she'd done something kind for Furbert in the midst of her own grief heightened his regard for her even more.

Max stirred the turkey, unsure of what to say. She'd been so emotional earlier in the day, he didn't know what to make of her preternaturally calm demeanor now.

"What are you making?"

"Lasagna for us. Turkey and rice for Furbert."

"Oh."

"Is that okay? I'll make sure to replace the groceries I use for him." He didn't want her to think he and his dog were going to eat her out of house and home.

"It's not a problem," she said, waving away his concern. "I just didn't realize he could eat people food."

"Yeah." Max relaxed, relieved he hadn't upset her. "There are some foods that are good for him, and a lot that isn't. But meat and rice is a nice treat for him."

Molly watched him quietly. He couldn't read her expression, but she seemed almost…normal. If he hadn't known about the events of the day, he'd have thought she was simply in a contemplative mood.

She said something, though she spoke so quietly he couldn't hear. "What's that?" he asked as he dumped the turkey and the rice in a large bowl and began stirring.

Molly gave him a small smile. "I was just saying you look good in the kitchen. A real natural."

Max laughed, though her words worried him a bit. He still wasn't sure how they were going to work things out between them. The news of Sabrina's murder had cast a pall over everything, dulling the earlier sense of urgency they'd both felt to come up with a plan.

He wasn't going to leave Molly and the baby in the lurch—that much he knew. But he also still knew he wasn't cut out for marriage. It would be better for both of them if Molly didn't get any ideas about domestic bliss, since that was one thing he couldn't give her.

The oven timer dinged, saving him from having to reply. He set Furbert's food next to the water bowl, then retrieved the lasagna. Molly grabbed some plates and silverware, setting the table as he put the lasagna on the table and fetched them drinks. They moved well together in this kitchen ballet, which Max found surprising. He'd never achieved this kind of synchronicity with Beth, not even in the early days of their marriage when they'd still been madly in love. Joint ventures in the kitchen had always resulted in them bumping into each other, and not in a deliberate, flirtatious way.

*Maybe that should have been my first clue*, he mused as he sat across from Molly.

"Thanks for cooking," she said.

"It's the least I could do." He picked up his fork and dug in. The sounds from across the room told him Furbert was enjoying his meal, as well. Molly didn't really eat, though—she pushed the food around on her plate but didn't seem to take a bite.

"Not hungry?" he asked.

She lifted one shoulder in a shrug. "Not especially."

"What about Little Bit?"

The corners of her lips lifted. "Is that what you're calling her?"

Max ducked his head, feeling his cheeks heat. In truth, the name had just popped out. He hadn't meant to assign a nickname to the baby, but it felt right. "I guess so."

"I like it. It's sweet."

He looked up to find her smiling at him. He smiled back, pleased to see her take a real bite of food.

They ate in companionable silence. It felt nice to just sit with her, to be in her presence and not feel like he needed to talk. He was used to schmoozing potential donors or eating with his team of administrators, meals that involved constant conversation with very little quiet time for reflection or thought. The need to be "on" all the time was exhausting, but it was a sacrifice he had to make for the good of K-9 Cadets. This simple dinner with Molly reminded him again of why he'd been drawn to her in the first place—there was a stillness about her that allowed him to relax. He never felt like he had to put on a show for her; the way she looked at him made him feel like he was enough, just the way he was.

Did he do the same for her? Did he bring her peace, allow her space and room to breathe? Hopefully so; surely she wouldn't have asked him to stay today if she were uncomfortable around him. She'd always been happy to see him before. At every visit, he'd loved to see her pretty blue eyes light up when she'd first catch sight of him. Her obvious pleasure had made him feel ten feet tall, and he'd done his best to show her how happy he was to see her, as well.

There was no denying they were good together. But now that they'd added a baby to the equation, how would that alter their chemistry?

Babies changed relationships. Several of his friends from the service had come home to a wife and new baby, only to find their marriage irrevocably different, and not always for the better. He knew three men alone who had gotten divorced in the first few years after adding a baby to the family. Their reasoning? "She's not the same person I married. Everything I do is wrong, and I'm tired of getting treated like a second child." These were men who had dedicated their adult lives to serving their country; they didn't make commitments lightly. For them to walk away like that meant things had to have been really bad.

As Max stole glimpses of Molly across the table,

worry began to nibble in earnest at the edges of his thoughts. She seemed the same to him now, her sister's death notwithstanding. But how would motherhood change her? How would fatherhood change him, for that matter? What if they turned into people who no longer recognized each other?

They couldn't put a child in the middle of that kind of uncertainty. It wasn't right. So where did that leave them?

"What's wrong?"

He looked up to find Molly studying him, her brow furrowed. "I was just thinking," he said.

"About the baby?"

Was she a mind reader? Or were his thoughts evident on his face? "That. And other things," he confessed.

"We have a lot to talk about," she replied.

He pushed his empty plate forward and leaned his elbows on the table. "Yes, we do." He felt his muscles tense as he braced himself to start this conversation.

"But not today." Her voice wavered slightly, betraying cracks in her composure.

"All right." Waiting wasn't going to make things any easier, but there was no need to address the elephant in the room now. Molly had dealt with enough today—he didn't need to add to her stress. "Whenever you're ready."

She traced her fork through the sauce on her plate. Max noticed she hadn't eaten much, but at least she'd taken a few bites.

"I don't know why I'm so tired," she said with a sigh. "I napped the afternoon away."

"Maybe it's for the best," he told her. "If you're asleep, you don't have to think." It was a strategy he'd used before, after the dissolution of his marriage. It had worked, too—for a little while.

Molly nodded. She pushed to her feet, reached for her plate.

Max jumped up. "Let me do that." He took the plate from her and gathered his own. "Why don't you go lie down?" She made a face at that suggestion, so he tried another one. "Maybe there's something mindless on television?"

"Maybe." She didn't sound excited by the prospect. "On second thought, I think I'll just go to bed." She stopped next to him, looking up hesitantly.

He could tell she wanted to say something, but wasn't sure how to go about it. "What is it?" He brushed a strand of hair away from her face, his fingertips caressing the shell of her ear. The contact sent sparks shooting up his arm, a potent reminder of their undeniable chemistry.

"I don't want to be alone tonight." The words spilled out of her, bouncing between them.

His heart kicked at the immediate implication of her confession, but he quickly quashed his baser impulses. She bit her lip and closed her eyes, clearly embarrassed.

"I'm sorry," she said. "I don't mean—"

"It's fine," he soothed, running his hand down her

arm. "I know what you're asking. And the answer is yes. I'll stay with you."

"Thank you." She offered him a grateful smile, her eyes shiny with tears.

"Don't mention it. Now go on. I'll get this cleaned up and join you in a few minutes."

Max watched her walk away, conflicting emotions swirling in his chest. He wanted to be there for her, to be the man she needed him to be. But past experiences had taught him he wasn't any good at relationships.

What, then, could he offer her?

And would it be enough?

Max moved carefully as he slid into bed a little later that evening. Molly appreciated his consideration, but he needn't have worried about disturbing her. She was awake, and likely would be for some time yet.

She was lying on her back, staring at the ceiling. A night-light in the hall just outside her bedroom provided a small glimmer of illumination in the dark, enough for her to see the blades of the ceiling fan spinning overhead.

Wanting a different view, she turned her head to look at Max, hoping to catch him with his eyes closed so she could study his face. She'd done that a lot when they'd first started seeing each other; some of her favorite moments with him had occurred while he was sleeping. She'd loved to watch him dream, see the play of unguarded expressions that crossed his face while he slumbered. He was so composed and controlled while awake, which made seeing him like this even more special. Max had shared his body with her, but by sleeping next to her, he'd also shared his soul.

She felt a little jolt as her eyes met his—she hadn't expected him to be watching her.

"Hi," he whispered.

"Hi," she whispered back.

He was lying on his side, his body several inches away from hers.

A sudden chill swept over her, making her shudder.

"Cold?"

"Yes," she said. The temperature of the room hadn't changed, but out of nowhere, her brain conjured up one of the pictures Deputy Sheriff Bloom had shown her earlier: the image of her sister's hair spread out on the steel table of the morgue.

Molly bit her lip, trying hard not to cry as she imagined the feel of the cold metal against her back. Even though the objective part of her brain knew Sabrina was dead and could no longer feel anything, it hurt to think of her sister lying alone on that unforgiving surface.

"Let me help." Max's voice was soft and soothing. His hands gently guided her onto her side, facing away from him. Then he slipped his arm around her waist and pulled her close, until her back was snug against his chest.

Molly immediately felt warmer, though the image

of Sabrina took longer to fade from her mind's eye. She focused on the feel of Max against her body, of the rise and fall of his chest as he breathed, the warm weight of his palm splayed across her baby bump.

His scent surrounded her, bringing her comfort with every breath she took. God, how she'd missed him these past few months! He was more than just her lover—somewhere along the way he'd become her best friend, and she'd missed the simple joy of talking to him. Her anger over his absence and lack of communication had drawn battle lines between them, but it didn't always have to be that way.

Molly was still trying to process Sabrina's death, but the loss of her sister was already making her think twice about Max and the baby. Life was too short; should she really spend it feeling hurt about what couldn't be, rather than grateful for what could?

Her hip was starting to ache; she shifted a bit to ease the pressure on the joint. The discomfort was a reminder of all the small ways pregnancy had made her feel like a stranger in her own body.

She moved again, bringing one knee up, then sliding her leg back down when that failed to provide relief. Maybe if she put a pillow between her knees…

"Molly?"

"Hmm?" she said absently.

"Can you, ah, stop wriggling?"

There was an odd note in Max's voice that made her pause. It was then that she felt a new sensation against her lower back.

"Oh," she said, understanding dawning at once.

"Sorry." He sounded sheepish. "I didn't mean to… well, it's just that you started moving, and I can't exactly control…" He released her and rolled onto his back. "Please don't take it the wrong way. I'm not trying to put the moves on you or anything."

The loss of his touch left her feeling bereft. Without stopping to think, Molly rolled over until she was facing him again. She placed her hand flat on his chest, her palm resting over his heart.

"It's okay," she said softly. "I don't mind."

She felt his heartbeat speed up. "What are you saying?"

"I'm saying that I'm tired of thinking. I just want to get out of my head right now. With everything that's happened recently, I can't stand to be in my own thoughts anymore."

She began to move her hand down his chest, feeling his muscles twitch in response to her touch. "I miss you," she whispered. "If I've learned anything over the past couple of days, it's that life is too short. I don't want to have any regrets."

Max placed his hand over hers, flattening it against the hard planes of his stomach. "I don't want you to have any regrets, either," he said, his voice husky. "Are you sure this is what you want? We still have so many unresolved issues between us. Won't this only complicate things even more?"

"Only if we let it," she said. "I'm not asking you for any promises. Can't we just have this moment out of time?" Molly struggled to find the words to explain her desperate need for a connection. The abyss of her grief yawned wide; if Max didn't pull her back from the edge, she feared she would topple over.

Max studied her face, his eyes dark shadows only a few inches from her own. "All right," he said softly. His breath ghosted across her lips, a prelude of what was to come. "Tell me what you want."

"You," she said, her voice cracking on the word. "I just want you."

It was all she'd wanted for the last year and a half, when she'd first felt herself start the downward slide into love. But she couldn't tell him that. This moment was an escape for both of them. They could talk about emotions later, when they returned to the real world. For now, she simply wanted to lose herself with Max, to shut off her brain and let her body take control.

Max traced his fingertip along the curve of her cheek, sending a shiver down Molly's spine. "All right," he said again. "You have me. I'm all yours."

*If only that were true.* She pushed the thought aside as Max drew her close, his hands on her skin awakening nerves that had gone dormant due to lack of use.

Soon, Molly was awash in sensation, clinging to Max and the promise of respite from her mind he provided. She didn't know what tomorrow would bring, or how things would change between them. All she had was this stolen moment with him, a chance to recapture their magic in the midst of terrible circumstances.

It would have to be enough.

# Chapter 11

"Everything looks good," Dr. Allen told Molly at her morning appointment, giving her a reassuring pat on the knee. "Your baby's right in the middle of the growth curve and shows no signs of being affected by your ordeal in the gondola."

Molly sighed, feeling a flash of relief. It was the first good news she'd heard since word of Sabrina's murder. And while she'd believed the OB from the hospital when he'd said the baby was fine, it was nice to have her regular doctor confirm it.

"I'm so glad," she said. "How big is she?"

Dr. Allen glanced at her tablet, which displayed the results from Molly's earlier ultrasound. "Looks like about fourteen ounces, give or take a few. She's about as long as a banana right now."

"That doesn't seem very big." It was the first time Max had spoken, aside from introducing himself to Dr. Allen.

"Don't worry—she won't stay little for long. She's going to keep putting on weight, and toward the end of the pregnancy, she'll grow by about half a pound a week."

"I'm okay with small," Molly said quickly.

Dr. Allen laughed. "That's what all my patients say." She stood, offered her hand to Molly and then Max. "I'll see you next month. Call my office if you need anything before then." She turned to Max. "It was nice to meet you."

"Same here," he said. "Thanks, Doctor."

"My pleasure."

The door *snicked* shut behind her, leaving Molly and Max alone once more. She glanced over at him—he was studying the clutch of ultrasound pictures they'd been given after the scan, a slight frown on his face.

"What's wrong?"

"I hate to say it, but I think she might have my nose." He flipped a photo around, tapping the profile image that showed the curves of the baby's face.

Molly laughed. "It's a little early to tell, but you might be right."

"Poor girl," he muttered, shaking his head.

"There are worse things in life than having your nose." In fact, Molly thought his nose was rather cute, but she didn't think he'd be happy to hear it.

He helped her slide off the table, and they walked through the office, headed for the parking lot.

It was a sunny day, the sky a pale, perfect blue. Molly glanced at the mountain as they walked toward her car. The avalanche had left a gash in the snowpack on the mountain, a scar that would eventually disappear when winter brought fresh powder to the area. The poles that supported the gondola lines looked like dark toothpicks from this distance, and she saw a few tiny brightly clad dots moving around—the workers who continued to assess the system, making repairs to get it operational again.

She shuddered, remembering all too well the terror of hanging precariously in the air, fearing that with each gust of wind they would plummet to the ground.

"Doing okay?" Max eyed her curiously over the roof of the car.

"Fine," she said. "Just having a flashback to the other day."

"That was pretty scary," he agreed. "Even for me. And I've voluntarily jumped out of perfectly good airplanes before."

Molly slid into the passenger seat as Max got behind the wheel. "I had no idea you were scared," she said. "You seemed so calm the whole time, like it was an inconvenience to your day, but nothing to be afraid of."

"I was putting on a brave face for you," he admitted. His cheeks turned pink as he ducked his head. "I knew you were scared, and I didn't want to make it worse. I figured if I acted like everything was okay, it would help you feel better."

His confession gave her a warm fuzzy feeling inside. "It did," she told him. She wanted to reach over and take his hand, but wasn't sure how he'd respond.

Her mind flashed back to last night, and Max's tenderness as they'd made love. He'd seemed to understand her need for touch, her desire for reassurance they were still alive. She'd told him she didn't want anything from him, and that had been the truth. But against her best intentions, she'd given him another piece of her heart.

She was glad he'd come to her doctor's appointment, as well. His interest in the baby made her feel good, and she took it as a positive sign for their future. In fact, if the time they'd spent together lately was any indication, they wouldn't have too much trouble adjusting to living together if things worked out between them.

"When are your parents getting into town?"

The question cast a pall over her thoughts. "They should be here by Friday," she said. They'd been in eastern Canada when she'd called, so it was going to take several days for them to make the drive home. In the meantime, Mason had actually volunteered to make the funeral arrangements, a task Molly appreciated him claiming.

"It's the least I can do," he'd said yesterday. "Since I made you break the news to Mom and Dad alone."

Molly hadn't pointed out the fact that Max had

actually been with her during the call. She'd simply said thanks and offered to help if he needed it.

"I know I said I'd give you time, but we do need to start talking about what comes next." Max kept his gaze on the road as he drove them through town.

Molly's shoulders tensed, though there was nothing negative about his tone. "All right," she said. "What are your thoughts?"

His grip on the wheel tightened, the knuckles of his fingers going white before he relaxed again. "I want you to know that I will absolutely support the baby, no matter what happens between us."

Molly nodded. "Thank you," she said quietly. It was an outcome she hadn't taken for granted, and it took some of the weight off her mind to know that Max would financially contribute to the expenses of raising a child.

"Of course." He fell silent, and after a few seconds, Molly realized he wasn't going to say more.

"How do you think this is going to work?" she prodded. "How often do you think you'll see the baby?"

"I'm not sure," he admitted. "A lot of it depends on K-9 Cadets, and how frequently I'll be able to break away for a visit."

Molly's heart sank at his words. Without necessarily meaning to, Max had dashed any hopes she'd had that they might stay together as a family. She closed her eyes, trying to prevent tears from welling up.

"So there's no way you can run the charity from here?"

He sighed. "I suppose it's possible, but…"

"But what?"

"I don't think that's such a good idea."

"Why?" Before he could answer, Molly felt a dam break free inside her, and her words spewed out in a torrent. "Why can't you stay here? Why can't we try to be a family? We're good together, you and I. We've always had a connection, don't you think?"

"Yes, but—"

"But what?" Frustration bubbled up inside her, finding a release as she raised the volume of her voice. "I've never felt so comfortable with anyone before, Max. And these past few days showed me that the magic between us isn't confined to the fun of your visits—it's there in the everyday tasks, the mundane. Even the bad," she said, her thoughts on Sabrina. She shook her head, focusing on the here and now. "Why can't we just try to be together for real?"

"I tried that before, Molly," he said, his voice tight. "It didn't work."

"She cheated on you!" Molly couldn't believe he was going to punish her for the actions of his ex-wife. "Do you honestly think I would ever do that to you?"

"No. But that's not the point."

"Oh? Well, enlighten me, please." Anger was burning away her frustration, loosening her tongue. "If you don't think the worst of me, then why aren't you willing to give us a shot?"

"Because I don't have it in me!" Max pulled into her garage and jerked the car into Park. He turned to face her, his green eyes blazing. "Beth didn't cheat on me because she was a bad person, but because I left her alone in our marriage. Apparently, I'm only good for one thing at a time, and right now that's K-9 Cadets."

Molly stared at him, unable to believe what she was hearing. "That is the biggest load of crap I've ever heard in my life."

Max looked away. "It's the truth."

"No, it's not. Your ex-wife told you that to justify her actions. And for some reason, you believed her. Probably because you felt guilty about being gone so much. But believe me, Beth's actions were her own. No one made her cheat on you, least of all you."

"You don't understand." His voice was low, barely audible in the stillness of the car.

Molly shook her head, a sense of finality washing over her. "You're right… I don't." She climbed out of the car and headed for the door. After a few seconds, she heard the car door slam and knew Max was following her.

She stepped aside to let him unlock the door, then took the keys from his hand. Pushing inside the house, she walked past Furbert and dropped her purse on the kitchen table. When she looked back, Max was standing in the doorway, Furbert at his feet.

"You do what you think is best, Max," she said, reaching for a glass. "I'm not going to beg you to be with me." She filled the glass with water, took a sip to ease the ache in her throat. "But know this— things have changed now. I'm not going to let you pop in and out of my life whenever you feel like it.

That was fun for a time, but I deserve more. And so does our daughter."

"I know that."

"Good."

He was quiet a moment, then asked, "What happens now?"

She made a shooing gesture with her hand. "Go home, back to your work. Just don't expect me to take you back when you decide in a few years that you're missing out on the most important parts of life." Her hand came to rest on her belly, her tone defiant.

Max studied her for a moment. "It doesn't have to be all or nothing," he said tersely.

"It does for me," Molly said. "I need more than a part-time partner."

He looked down, clenching his teeth. "Fair enough."

"Besides, do you honestly think you can be a drop-in dad to this baby?"

"You make it sound so terrible." Max looked up, took a step closer. "Why can't I have it both ways? Why can't I run my charity and visit my daughter on a regular basis? I could fly out here once a month, stay for a week at a time. What's wrong with that?"

She nearly laughed at his suggestion. "I'm sure it would start out that way," she replied. "But how long would it take before you got so busy you missed a trip? Just one at first. But as your organization expanded, or you needed to raise more funds, it would get easier and easier for you to push those visits aside. Then, you'll turn around and it will have been six months since you've seen her, or a year. Finally, you'll decide you may as well not come at all, since it's already been so long."

Max didn't reply. But she could tell by the expression on his face he'd heard her.

"That's not fair to this baby," she said quietly.

"So what are you saying?" His voice was flat, emotionless. "That you want me to walk away? That if I'm not willing to give you everything you want, I may as well stay out of your lives completely? I never thought you were one for issuing ultimatums." He crossed his arms, glaring at her.

"I'm not," Molly replied evenly. "I will never keep you from seeing your daughter. But I won't let you disappoint her, either."

"She's my baby, too," he said, a warning glint in his eyes.

"Then I guess you'd better do right by her," Molly said. "Hopefully you won't let your hang-ups about commitment ruin your relationship with her the way they did ours."

Max shook his head, dropped his arms. "This is getting us nowhere."

"On the contrary," she shot back. "I think it's been quite illuminating." Her heart was breaking in two, but at least now she knew where she stood with Max.

Or didn't, as the case was.

He drew in a deep breath, his chest expanding with the effort. "I'm going to go for now. But I'm not leaving town yet. As far as I'm concerned, we still have a lot to iron out."

"Really? Because it seems to me we've already covered all of the important stuff. The rest is just details. I'm sure your secretary is more than capable of handling those. I know how hard it is for you to do the little things, like returning emails or phone calls."

Max flinched, and Molly immediately felt guilty for the dig. She had promised not to punish him forever for that mistake. But her intentions were no match for her roiling emotions at the moment.

Max nodded. "I suppose I deserved that." He took a step back, glanced down. "Come on, boy," he said to Furbert. "Time for us to go."

Furbert got to his feet, looking as worried as possible for a dog. He glanced between Max and Molly, as if hoping one of them would explain what was happening.

Molly followed Max and the dog down the hall, intending to lock up after them. But just as she stepped forward to shut the front door, Max whirled on his heel, bringing them face-to-face.

"I wasn't lying earlier, Molly," he said. His breath was warm on her cheek, his eyes flashing green fire. "I will be back. We aren't finished here."

"You'll forgive me if I don't hold my breath." She shut the door before he could reply, realizing only after she did so that he had no way to get back to The Lodge. For a split second, she considered letting him back in and calling for a cab, but decided against it. He could walk into town, or call Blaine for a ride if he was feeling lazy. Either way, she wasn't going to worry about it.

Emotions rattled inside her, bouncing around like bees in a bottle. Molly forced herself to walk into the den, sit on the sofa. It felt strange to be alone after being around Max and Furbert all weekend. The house seemed so much bigger without the two of them there.

The adrenaline from the argument faded, leaving her feeling hollowed out and heartsick. Unable to think of anything else to do, Molly lay down on the couch. Staring up at the ceiling, she surrendered to her tears.

"Why, Deputy Sheriff Bloom, how nice it is to see you."

The booming voice stopped Daria in her tracks. She'd stopped in the diner for a quick bite to eat, and had seen the mayor and Russ Colton walk in together. She'd quickly finished her lunch and started for the door, hoping to avoid talking to them. But it seemed she wasn't going to make a clean getaway after all.

She turned and offered a smile to both men. "Nice to see you, Mayor. Mr. Colton."

"You, as well." Mayor Dylan smiled up at her. "Do you have a minute? I'd love to bend your ear."

It wasn't really a question, and they both knew it. She nodded, pulling out one of the free chairs at their table.

Russ Colton sat across from her, a glass of tea in

his hand. "Hell of a thing, that avalanche," he said, turning to glance out the windows of the diner. "We were lucky no one was hurt."

"Yes, sir," Daria replied. She studied his face as he took a sip from his glass, searching for her adoptive father's features in his own. Joe Colton, former president of the United States, had adopted her when she was very young. He and his wife had been loving parents, and Daria had wanted for nothing while growing up. But Daria needed to make a name for herself based on her own merits, not because of her connection to her father. So she'd changed her last name back to Bloom and set off in search of her biological family in the hopes of learning more about them and her past. The trail had led her to Colorado, and Daria had fallen in love with the area. She'd settled in Roaring Springs, learning only after the fact that the Colton family's reach extended here, as well.

No one had discovered her secret...yet. And she intended to keep it that way. Most of the Coltons in town were nice—she certainly had nothing bad to say about Trey Colton, the sheriff and her boss—but Daria was quite happy to remain on the fringes of their lives, apart from the drama inherent in such a large family.

Mayor Dylan leaned forward. "I'll get right to the point, Deputy Sheriff. What's going on with those bodies?"

"We're still investigating," she began, but he interrupted.

"Yes, yes, of course. But I was hoping you had

some new information to share. Have you been able to identify anyone yet?"

She glanced meaningfully at Russ Colton, hesitating. Mayor Dylan waved away her silent inquiry.

"You can speak freely in front of Russ."

Daria wasn't so sure about that, but she couldn't very well contradict the mayor in front of the most powerful businessman in town.

"We have positive confirmation that one of the bodies is that of Sabrina Gilford." She was confident one of the other bodies belonged to April Thomas, a young woman who had been missing for over a year, and whose mother had come to town a few months ago searching for her. But Daria was keeping her thoughts to herself on that one until the forensic results were in.

A shadow crossed Russ's face; Sabrina was his niece. Daria didn't think Russ had been an especially doting uncle, but the news had likely come as a shock.

"I had heard that," the mayor said. "But what about the others?"

"We're still in the process of trying to make identifications. We've sent the remains to the state lab in Denver. Some of the bodies are in advanced stages of decomposition, making the process more difficult."

Mayor Dylan nodded, running his hand down his face. "I see."

"I'm happy to keep your office updated on the progress of my investigation," she offered, hoping to put an end to this conversation.

"I'd appreciate that," the mayor said. "Do you think this is the work of a serial killer?"

"I do, yes." Both the mayor and Russ Colton gaped at her, as if they'd been expecting a different answer. "Six bodies buried in the same location is not a coincidence."

"No, I suppose it's not." Dylan frowned. "Do you think he's still here?"

"If it is indeed a he, I imagine he's still around, yes. Ms. Gilford hasn't been dead for very long. That suggests whoever killed these women is still active in the area."

"My God." The mayor leaned back in his chair, shaking his head in disbelief. "Here in Roaring Springs."

"I'm afraid so," she confirmed. Daria glanced at her watch; she really needed to get back to the station. Hopefully the mayor would let her go soon.

"What are you going to tell the public?"

*Ah*, she thought. *That's why he wanted to talk to me.* "I'm going to tell them what we know so far. We're obviously not going to release all the information we have, but the fact that we discovered six bodies here is national news."

Mayor Dylan frowned again, clearly unhappy that word of the gruesome find had spread beyond Roaring Springs. "Be that as it may, I think you should downplay the serial killer angle."

Daria lifted one brow. "Mr. Mayor, with all due respect, I don't have to say the words *serial killer*.

The press is only too happy to speculate about that without any input from me."

"But you can help shape their reports," he insisted. "The way you react to their questions will determine how sensationalistic their angle becomes. If you make it seem like you agree with the idea there's a serial killer using Roaring Springs as his hunting ground, that will turn into the story."

"It seems to me that *is* the story," she replied.

"But you can't be sure the victims are all connected until the medical examiner has finished his work."

Daria conceded his point with a nod.

Dylan leaned forward, planting his elbows on his knees. "Listen, I know you have a job to do. And I'm not in any way trying to stifle your investigation. But the film festival is scheduled to begin soon. You know how much money that puts in the town's coffers."

*And your friend's as well*, Daria thought to herself. Russ was the CEO of the Colton Empire, the name his father had given to the corporation that encompassed The Lodge and The Chateau, two locations that were always sold out during the annual film festival. Daria knew several of Russ's children, as well as some of his nieces and nephews, also had local businesses in town or nearby. The Colton family was so entwined with Roaring Springs that anything that was good for the area was good for their bottom line, too.

"If the media get fixated on the idea of a serial

killer here," the mayor continued, "people will start to worry. They might decide the film festival isn't worth the risk of staying here. If the festival goes under, that'll be the end of it. The town won't be able to recoup that lost income, and the festival itself will likely never be successful again. We can't let that happen."

Daria sighed quietly. She understood the point the man was making, and his concerns for the town. But she had to balance his worries about money with the very real possibility that greater publicity about this case would generate more leads for her to follow as people contacted the department with tips. These five unidentified women, whoever they were, hadn't been invisible. People around town had seen them, talked to them. Someone out there likely had information that could help Daria catch the killer. But if the mayor insisted she keep things quiet, she might never get to hear it.

"A certain amount of publicity is a good thing," she began, hoping to explain her reasoning and draw the mayor to her side.

Dylan was having none of it. "I'm asking you this as a favor," he said, though his tone made it clear that was far from the truth. "Roaring Springs cannot afford this scandal right now. By all means, continue your investigation. But do it quietly."

Daria took a deep breath, then nodded. Agreeing with the mayor was the only way she was going to get out of this conversation. Besides, his request made a certain kind of sense.

"All right. I won't emphasize the possibility we have a serial killer in the area."

He smiled broadly, pleased to have won.

"But," she continued, causing his smile to freeze, "I won't ignore those questions, either. I understand your concerns about the film festival and the financial future of this town. But I have a responsibility to protect the residents of Roaring Springs. At some point, they will need to know if there is a predator in their midst."

"Of course, of course," Dylan said, his tone syrupy sweet. He stood, clasping his hands together as he leaned forward. "And believe me, I will do everything in my power to help you keep this town safe. I just think it's best you not draw any premature conclusions before all the forensic data is available."

"Fair enough, Mayor." Daria managed to keep the edge out of her voice. She didn't need him telling her how to do her job, but it was easier to play nice. "I'll be in touch."

She rose and shook hands with both men. "I look forward to hearing from you soon," Dylan said. "Be sure to let me know if my office can assist your investigation in any way."

Daria nodded. "Thank you, sir," she said, knowing the diners at nearby tables were openly watching them. The last thing Daria wanted was for rumors to start swirling that there was bad blood between the mayor and the sheriff's department.

She headed to the parking lot, pulling out her cell phone as she walked. The lab guys probably didn't have any new results to report, but it wouldn't hurt to check. The mayor wasn't known for his patience—it was only a matter of time before he called her, wanting updates on the case. It would make her life easier if she had something to tell him.

## Chapter 12

Molly applied the last strip of painter's tape to the frame around the door on Wednesday morning and took a step back, eyeing her handiwork. She'd never painted a whole room before, but the guy at the hardware store had walked her through the basics and she'd followed his instructions. Now that the trim in the room was protected by blue strips of tape, she could start on the walls.

Transforming the guest bedroom into a nursery was going to be a big job. Molly was ready to throw herself into the project; hopefully, it would serve as a good distraction from the rest of the world.

She walked over to the paint can and tray in the middle of the floor and knelt, reaching for the opener.

But just as she fit the metal tool under the lid, someone knocked on her front door.

Her first instinct was to ignore the sound. She wasn't in the mood for company, especially not Max. He might think there was more that needed to be said, but as far as Molly was concerned, she'd heard enough yesterday.

Max had made it very clear that they didn't have a future together. And while he might think he could swoop in and spend time with the baby whenever his schedule allowed, Molly knew that arrangement wasn't going to last long. He'd already blown her off, and that was for a trip he took only four times a year. If he thought he was going to fly out here once a month, he was either delusional or lying to himself.

Molly felt like the biggest fool. She'd gotten involved with Max knowing he was only good for a fling. But somewhere along the way, she'd made the mistake of falling for him. Then she'd compounded her mistake by thinking he felt the same way about her. She'd convinced herself they could be a family, that the two of them could find happiness together as they raised their child.

She certainly knew better now.

The knocking persisted. Molly got to her feet with a sigh. She wasn't going to be able to paint the nursery in peace with that racket going on in the background. Might as well open the door and tell Max to leave; otherwise, he was liable to stand there all day.

She flung open the door, ready to send him on

his way. But it wasn't Max who stood on her welcome mat.

It was Elaine.

"Oh," Molly said dumbly. "It's you."

Elaine smiled, though it didn't reach her eyes. "Hello," she said. "I was hoping to talk to you."

"Now's not really a good time," Molly hedged. She couldn't handle another verbal attack right now, not while she was still trying to process Sabrina's death and Max's rejection. Her poor heart simply couldn't take any more.

"Please? I'll only stay a moment." There was something subdued, almost broken about her that softened Molly's resolve. *She's suffering, too.*

"All right." Molly nodded and stepped back, holding open the door for Elaine.

She led her into the living room and sat on the sofa, gesturing to the chair. "Can I get you something to drink?" she offered automatically.

Elaine sank onto the chair, clutching her purse to her chest as though she feared someone was going to jump out from around the corner to snatch it.

"No, I'm fine."

"How's Mason?" Molly hadn't spoken to him since yesterday afternoon. Apparently, the police weren't going to release Sabrina's body anytime soon, so he'd put the funeral planning on hold. He'd still sounded tired, and Molly worried he wasn't getting enough rest.

"He's stressed," Elaine confirmed. "He's working so hard to help organize the film festival, but he hasn't been sleeping. He says every time he closes his eyes, he sees Sabrina's face."

"Oh, God," Molly said, understanding the problem far too well. Her thoughts were dominated by her sister and Max; neither subject brought much comfort right now. "He can't go on like this. Maybe his doctor can give him something to help him sleep?"

"I'm going to call his office and ask," Elaine replied. "But that's not actually why I stopped by."

"Oh? What's on your mind?"

Elaine scooted forward until she sat perched on the edge of her seat. "I've been doing a lot of thinking, and I've figured out a solution for your issue." She nodded meaningfully at Molly's belly.

She felt her hackles rise. "I didn't realize I had an 'issue.'"

Elaine continued as if she hadn't heard her. "The way I see it, this baby is coming at a bad time for you. You clearly weren't planning on it, and I don't think you're ready to be a mother. But I am."

Molly stared at Elaine, too stunned to speak. Was she actually proposing Molly hand over her daughter?

Apparently mistaking her silence for interest, Elaine carried on, the words flowing faster as her excitement ratcheted up. "Mason and I can't have children. But we want so desperately to be parents. Why don't you let us adopt your baby? That way, your life can carry on as normal, and we can complete our family."

Her plea tugged at Molly's heartstrings. Not because she was interested in giving up her child, but because it was clear Elaine was emotionally invested in this idea.

"Elaine, I—" she began, but the other woman cut her off.

"It really is the perfect solution. Mason would have a child he's biologically connected to, and we would love the baby like it was our own."

"What does Mason think of this idea?" Molly needed to know if her brother was on board with this preposterous plan, or if it was something Elaine had come up with on her own.

Her sister-in-law looked away. "He doesn't know about it. I was hoping to surprise him with the good news."

That made Molly feel a little bit better. At least her brother didn't seem to have designs on her baby.

"Elaine," she said, feeling her way into a response. It was clear the other woman was in a fragile mental state. Molly didn't want her rejection to make things worse, but she had to make it clear she had no intention of giving up her baby. "I appreciate the offer. It's clear you've put a lot of thought into this, and I know you're coming from a place of love."

Elaine nodded, her smile bordering on manic.

"So that's a yes?"

Molly shook her head. "No, it's not. I know your heart is in the right place, but I'm not interested in putting my baby up for adoption."

"But…" Elaine's smile slipped. "But you can't possibly mean that! It would be the best thing for everyone! You don't want to be a single mother, and Mason and I can give the baby everything!"

"I know it will be hard doing things on my own, but I'm prepared to make sacrifices." Molly got to her feet. She was done talking to Elaine about her baby. It was clear the other woman was struggling with her own demons, and while Molly felt for her, she didn't have the emotional energy to help her.

"No." Elaine shook her head, as if she could change Molly's mind through sheer force of will. "No, you just need to give it more thought."

Recognizing the futility of trying to argue with her, Molly instead focused on getting the other woman out of her house. "Elaine, as I said before, I'm really busy. I need you to leave now, please." *And I need to call Mason.* She knew her brother was already overwhelmed, but he needed to know his wife was becoming unhinged.

Elaine got to her feet, one hand digging in her bag. Molly assumed she was fumbling for her car keys, but when she withdrew her hand, she wasn't gripping a key chain.

She was holding a gun.

Molly took a step back, her heart jumping into her throat. "Elaine…"

"I didn't want to have to do this," her sister-in-law said. "But you leave me no choice."

"Please, put the gun down," Molly cajoled, her voice shaking. "This isn't necessary."

"Apparently, it is. Now come on." She gestured

to the hall, clearly expecting Molly to accompany her somewhere.

"No." If she went with Elaine, she was as good as dead.

In response, Elaine cocked the gun. The sound turned Molly's guts to water. "Move."

Molly's legs wobbled as she took a step. "What are you going to do? If you kill me, the baby dies, too."

"I know that." Elaine urged her toward the door. "I'm not going to kill you. Not yet, anyway."

"Then what—" Molly stopped before the door, trying to stall. Elaine dug the muzzle of the gun into her lower back, pressing so hard against her that Molly cried out.

"Don't get any ideas," she warned. "I want you alive, but I can still make you hurt if you don't do what I say." She reached past Molly and threw open the door, then shoved Molly forward.

"My car," she directed.

Gun at her back, Molly had no choice but to do as she was told.

"You don't have to do this," she said, glancing around as she walked down the porch steps. Her home was set back a bit from the street, in a small grove of trees. Normally, Molly enjoyed the privacy. Now she wished her neighbors could see what was happening.

"I tried to do things the easy way," Elaine reminded her. "You didn't want to cooperate."

The car beeped softly as she unlocked it. She herded Molly into the passenger seat, then trotted around the hood and climbed behind the wheel. She placed the gun in her lap. Molly breathed a little easier now that it was no longer pointed at her, but she wasn't out of the woods yet. Maybe she could distract Elaine and grab the gun? She thought about simply lunging for it, but Elaine wasn't going to give it up without a fight. Molly couldn't risk the baby getting shot in the struggle.

Elaine caught her eye. "Don't even think about it," she warned.

Molly decided to try a different tack. "Think about what you're doing here. It's not too late to let me go back inside. We can forget this ever happened."

Elaine stuck the key in the ignition and turned. "We're past that now," she said.

It was horrifyingly clear to Molly that her sister-in-law was planning on stealing her baby. "What are you going to tell Mason?" she asked. "You can't just show up with a baby and expect him to accept it with no questions."

A shadow crossed Elaine's face, and Molly realized she hadn't thought that far ahead. "Put away the gun and let's just talk. I'm happy for you and Mason to be involved in the baby's life—parties, sleepovers, you name it." It would be a cold day in hell before Molly let Elaine anywhere near her child, but the other woman didn't need to know that right now. "We can all be one big happy family."

"Sunday dinners and walks in the park?" Elaine sounded wistful.

Molly nodded. "Absolutely. All of it."

Elaine looked at her, a glint of sadness in her green eyes. Then Molly's head snapped back, her nose exploding in burst of pain that had her seeing stars.

"Do you think I'm stupid?"

Molly grabbed her nose, squinting through tears as Elaine screamed, "I know you're only trying to get me to let you go. It's not going to work. Now shut up before I do something you'll really regret."

Molly slouched against the window, too dazed to react. The scenery passed by in a blur as Elaine stepped on the gas. Molly's hands felt warm; she pulled them away from her nose, noting with a sense of detachment that her palms were slick with blood.

"Don't touch anything!" Elaine snapped.

Molly didn't respond. She tried to pay attention to where they were going, but Elaine turned onto an old logging road that took them into the forest.

"Put this over your head." Something soft landed in Molly's lap. A pillowcase.

She hesitated, only to hear the gun cock again. "Don't make me ask you again."

Molly tugged the fabric over her face, her view of the outside world disappearing. If she'd thought things were bad before, the loss of visual cues made it worse. Every breath she took remained trapped in the folds of the fabric, making her feel light-headed. Her nose throbbed with every beat of her heart, and a trickle of blood ran over her lips and down her chin to drip onto her shirt.

Claustrophobia reared its ugly head; Molly pushed down the panic, knowing if she started to cry she wouldn't be able to breathe. Better to conserve her strength for later. She wanted to protect her baby, but that didn't mean she was going to let Elaine treat her like a lamb being led to slaughter. She'd cooperate for now, but Elaine had to leave her alone sometime. That was when she'd make her escape.

Her life—and that of her baby—depended on it.

"Am I crazy?"

Furbert cocked one ear in Max's direction, but otherwise didn't move. Max sighed, feeling disgusted with himself.

"Of course I am. Who the hell asks a dog that kind of question?"

Furbert let out a soft woof of agreement, then closed his eyes again with a sigh. Max shook his head. If only he could rest as peacefully as his dog.

He hadn't slept much last night. Every time he closed his eyes, he saw Molly's face, her expression a mixture of hurt and betrayal. *I did that to her*, he thought. *I caused that pain*.

It made him feel like the lowest of the low, knowing he'd let her down. And truly, if there were any other way, he would have embraced it with open arms. But he just couldn't be all that she needed him to be. The recognition of that fact filled him with shame, and he'd spent most of the night and all of the morning wrestling with his shortcomings.

The heart of the issue was that he *wanted* to be

the one for her—her partner, her lover, her friend. If he was being honest with himself, he'd even go so far as to say he wanted to be her husband. But he felt like a little kid with empty pockets, nose pressed up against the glass of the toy store, gazing longingly at what he wanted but couldn't have.

"She thinks she wants me." He shoved off the sofa and began to pace, the movement helping him think. Little did Molly know that if he committed to her, she'd soon grow tired of him and his divided loyalties. Beth had hated K-9 Cadets from the start; it only stood to reason Molly would soon grow to hate it, too, since it consumed so much of his time.

So no, Molly didn't actually want him. She wanted the *idea* of him. During his visits, it had been easy to shut out the world and pretend they were the only two people on the planet. The seclusion had made life seem better than it really was—after all, they'd deliberately ignored the problems and stresses of daily life, focusing instead on each other. It was a nice way to live, but it couldn't last.

And while he agreed with Molly that they were great together, he worried that the strength of their connection would fade when tested against the slings and arrows of everyday living. Would she still think he was funny when he forgot to put gas in the car? Would he still find her irresistible when she didn't pick up her shoes?

They'd had a great run together, there was no denying it. And though there was a small part of him that wanted to take the leap and see how they fared going forward, a larger part of him thought they might be better off leaving their relationship in the past. They would always be connected, thanks to the baby. But that didn't mean he had to continue to indulge in his feelings for Molly.

"It's for her own good," he told himself. He marched into the kitchen, poured another cup of coffee. Molly didn't realize it now, but he was doing her a favor.

It was for his own good, as well. Now that he'd told her there was no future for them together, he could start getting a grip on his emotions. They were going to have to see each other a lot for the sake of their daughter—he needed to have his feelings under control so he didn't wind up pining over Molly for the rest of his life. Better to close that door and move forward with his life; if he continued to look back, he was liable to go mad.

"Right," he said to the empty kitchen. "That's sorted, then."

So why did he still feel at a loss?

No matter. He just had to keep moving. Draining his coffee, he set the mug in the sink. "Come on," he called to Furbert. "We're going out."

What better way to test his newfound resolve than by visiting Molly? She wasn't going to be happy to see him again, but he only had a few days left in town and he wanted to iron out the details of his visitation plan before he headed home. And yes, okay, he wanted to check on her. But his interest was strictly platonic; he simply wanted to make sure the woman carrying his child was feeling better.

Even though his heart still ached over leaving her so upset yesterday.

He walked into the living room to find Furbert still snoozing on the couch. "Seriously, dog, I mean it. We're going out now." Molly loved Furbert, Max knew that much. He wasn't about to show up at her house without him.

The dog yawned widely, then grudgingly hopped down. Max clipped a leash to his collar and grabbed his jacket. As they set off down the path to the main building of The Lodge, he pulled out his phone and called for a cab. Blaine wouldn't mind giving him a ride, but Max didn't want to involve his friend in his personal troubles, especially since Molly was the man's cousin. He'd just have the taxi drop him at Molly's house and call the guy back when he needed to leave.

Now if he could just figure out what to say…

# Chapter 13

The car jerked to a stop, causing the back of Molly's head to crash against the seat. She jumped as Elaine grabbed her hands.

"Hold still," Elaine snapped.

Something cold touched Molly's wrists—*handcuffs*, she realized, just as the metal rings snapped into place. She felt the car move as Elaine got out, and a few seconds later, a chilly gust of air blew across her when her door was opened.

"Let's go." The other woman grabbed her arm, half pulling, half dragging her from the car. Molly started walking, stumbling a bit over the uneven ground. Based on the crunch of their footsteps and the feel of the ground beneath her feet, Molly guessed they were in a gravel parking lot.

The fact did nothing to help her narrow down their location. There were a lot of places in Roaring Springs and the surrounding area that were unpaved. She couldn't use their travel time as a marker, either; even though she hadn't been able to see where they were going, Molly had registered the many turns Elaine had taken. Unless she missed her guess, they hadn't left Roaring Springs at all.

She felt a flicker of hope at the possibility she wasn't far from home. That meant help was nearby. All she had to do was escape.

They stopped; Molly heard the jingle of keys, followed by the squeak of door hinges. Elaine pushed her forward, her tight grip on Molly's arm the only thing keeping her upright as she stumbled over the threshold.

Their footsteps echoed as they walked, giving Molly the impression they were in a large, empty space. The air was still and cold; she couldn't smell anything but blood right now, but she was willing to bet the place had a musty scent to it.

After what seemed like an eternity, Elaine pushed her down. Molly felt an instant of panic as she fell, only to land on a thin mattress. While she caught her breath, Elaine fumbled at her ankles, snapping restraints into place. Suddenly, the pillowcase was yanked off her head.

Molly squinted as light flooded her eyes. After a few blinks, her vision cleared enough for her to register her surroundings.

She was in a warehouse office, a small room in an

otherwise cavernous space. A pane of glass looked out on the warehouse proper, presumably so the boss could keep an eye on things from the comfort of his chair. There was a rusty metal desk shoved against the wall opposite her, and a matching file cabinet to her left. She sat on a metal bed, the kind that were used in hospitals back in the day. The thin mattress was a poor cushion for the springs that held the bed frame together—Molly's butt already hurt from sitting there.

She glanced down to find that Elaine had hooked her ankle to one ring of a set of handcuffs. The other ring was attached to a chain that was anchored to the floor. There was a bucket next to the desk, but no other furnishings.

"Home sweet home," Elaine trilled.

"You can't be serious," Molly rasped. "You can't possibly mean to keep me here."

Elaine looked around. "Why not? You're inside, out of the elements."

"I'll freeze!" It was already decidedly chilly inside the office; the temperature would plummet once the sun set.

Elaine stepped to the file cabinet and tugged on a drawer. It opened with a metallic squeal of protest. She reached inside, then threw a blanket on the mattress. "Here you go."

Molly eyed the dingy fabric with alarm. "That won't be enough to keep me warm!"

"You'll be fine," Elaine said dismissively. "It'll be summer soon; you won't even need it then."

Panic began to claw up Molly's throat. "What about food? Water? Or do you mean to starve me to death?"

Elaine tapped the other drawers. "There are provisions in here. Water bottles, some rations. Prenatal vitamins." She laughed. "We need to make sure the baby gets everything it needs."

"Please," Molly said, her eyes welling with tears. "Please don't do this."

"I'll visit you, of course." Elaine carried on as if she hadn't heard a word of Molly's plea. "I'll restock your food and water every couple of days. And I have a handheld Doppler, so we can listen to the baby's heartbeat together."

She sounded excited, as if it was going to be a bonding activity for the two of them.

"You can't leave me here." Molly sniffed, the action sending a fresh jolt of pain through her nose. "What if something happens to you and you can't get back to me? I'll die, and so will the baby!" She knew Elaine didn't give a damn about her, but maybe she would reconsider this crazy plan for the sake of the baby?

Elaine's smile slipped, and for a second, Molly thought she might have actually gotten through to her. Then she shook her head slightly and took a step toward the office door. "I'll leave you to settle in now. Try to get some rest—I'll be back soon to check on you."

She stepped out of the office, her boot heels making a clipped sound on the cement floor of the warehouse. Molly stood and tried to follow, but drew up short as the handcuff bit into her ankle. "Elaine!" she called. "Please, don't leave me here!"

When her sister-in-law didn't answer, Molly screamed her name. But the other woman kept walking, her form growing smaller as she got closer to the door. Through her tears, Molly saw a blurry rectangle of bright light flash at the end of the warehouse. Then the door slammed shut, casting the space in dim grays once more.

She sank back onto the thin mattress, her chest heaving as she sobbed. "I'm so sorry, baby." She whispered the words over and over again as she held her belly between her hands. "I *will* get us out of here."

But…how?

She wasn't home.

Max frowned and knocked on the door one last time. But just like his previous knocks, this one went unanswered.

He pulled his phone from his pocket and dialed Molly's number. Maybe she was out running errands? If that was the case, he'd happily sit on the porch steps until she got back home.

The phone rang and rang, but Molly didn't answer.

Hmm. It wasn't like her to ignore his calls. Then again, she'd never been so angry with him before.

Worry tickled the base of his spine. He dialed Blaine.

"Have you heard from Molly today?"

"I don't even rate a proper greeting anymore?" Blaine joked.

Max tamped down his impatience. "Sorry. Hello. Have you heard from Molly recently?"

"No. Why?"

"I'm at her house, and she's not answering her door."

"Maybe she's not home."

Max rolled his eyes. "Yes, thank you, Sherlock. But she's not answering her phone, either. Can you call her?"

"Why do you need me to call her? If she's not picking up, she's not picking up."

Max sighed. Why couldn't Blaine just do what he asked without making a federal case about it? "We had a fight yesterday. I don't know if she's not answering the phone because it's me calling, or if she's not answering it at all."

"Ah." There was a world of knowing in Blaine's tone. "Gotcha. Stand by a minute… I'll give her a ring from my office phone."

Max heard his friend punching buttons. Then he spoke again. "So…what'd you fight about?"

"*Star Wars* versus *Star Trek*," Max drawled.

"Really?" Blaine sounded genuinely surprised.

"No," Max growled. "Of course not. What do you think we argued about?"

"I can guess," Blaine said. He was quiet for a second, then said, "Nope, she's not picking up. It went to voice mail."

His stomach flip-flopped as his concern for her

grew. "Listen, I know you probably think I'm over-reacting, but do you have a spare key for her house, or know someone who does?"

"You think something's wrong?" Blaine's tone was serious now, and he knew his friend was paying attention.

"I'm not sure," Max said. "I just have a gut feeling that things aren't right. What if she's sick and can't reach the phone? What if that bump on her head is more serious than the doctor thought?" Visions of Molly lying unconscious on the floor danced through his head, feeding his worry for her. "I guess I'm being extra paranoid now that I know about the baby, but I want to make sure they're both okay."

"I can understand that. Tell you what—if anyone has an extra key to her place, it's her brother Mason. I'll give him a call, tell him to head your way. You mind waiting there for him?"

"Nope. I'll park it on the porch steps until he gets here."

"All right. I'll call him now and text you his ETA."

"Thanks, man." Max felt a small measure of relief knowing Blaine was taking his concerns seriously. "I appreciate it."

"Don't mention it," the other man said. "Sit tight. We'll get to the bottom of this little mystery soon."

It was a good twenty minutes before Mason arrived at Molly's house. Max had long since given up sitting quietly on the porch steps and was pacing back and forth, wearing a rut in the floorboards in front of Molly's door. Furbert sat on the welcome mat, watching him patiently.

Molly's brother climbed down from the cab of his pickup truck and glared at him. The man looked like hell—his hair was disheveled, there were dark circles under his eyes, and it was clear he hadn't shaved in days. As he approached, Max noted the lines of strain around Mason's eyes and lips. When was the last time the man had slept?

"Thanks for meeting me here," he said.

Mason stopped a few feet away from Max. "So you're the one who got my sister pregnant." It wasn't a question. Mason's gaze traveled from the top of Max's head down to his shoes, clearly taking his measure.

"Ah, yes, that's me." This wasn't exactly how Max had envisioned meeting Molly's family. The disappointment in Mason's voice was evident; he didn't imagine her parents would be any more excited. Furbert moved to sit at his feet, a show of solidarity that Max appreciated under the circumstances.

"What are your intentions regarding my sister?"

"That's actually what I came to discuss with her," Max said, hoping to steer her brother to the issue at hand. "But Molly isn't answering her phone or the door."

"I know. Blaine told me." Mason's lips tightened. "That's not like her." He walked over to the door, rapped hard on the wood. When she didn't respond, he took his keys from his pocket.

"I'm only doing this because I want to make sure

she's okay," he said, tossing the words over his shoulder as he fit the key into the lock. "I'm not here to do you any favors."

"I understand," Max assured him. All he cared about was making sure Molly and the baby were fine. He and Mason could work on their differences later.

Mason pushed the door open. "Molly?" he called out loudly. There was no response, so the two men and dog entered the house.

Max knew right away she wasn't there. The space had an empty feel to it, and the air was still. Mason called her name a few more times, but it was clear she wasn't going to respond.

They checked all the rooms, just to be sure. Max lingered a moment in the doorway of the guest bedroom, which had been taped in preparation for painting. There was a can of paint, a tray and a roller in the center of the room. He saw a pink smudge on the label of the can and realized with a jolt that Molly was starting work on the baby's nursery.

*She shouldn't be painting in her condition.* He wasn't an expert, but surely inhaling paint fumes while pregnant was a bad idea. *This should be my job.*

Out of nowhere, a sense of longing struck him. He wanted to be the one to help Molly put the nursery together, to assemble the crib, to hang the curtains. He wanted to pick out blankets and stuffed animals and clothes, to compare playpens and swings and car seats and help her shop for all the million things babies seemed to need.

Mason came to stand next to him, peering into the room. "I guess this is going to be the nursery." He spied the supplies on the floor. "She probably went to the hardware store for something."

"Maybe," Max said. But he wasn't convinced. Something about the house felt wrong, though he couldn't put his finger on what.

"Come on," Mason said, walking away. "I'm sure she'll be back soon, and she won't be happy to discover we've let ourselves in."

Max reluctantly began to follow Molly's brother. "Don't you find it strange she isn't answering her phone?"

Mason shrugged. "Maybe she just doesn't feel like talking to anyone right now."

It was a reasonable explanation, especially given the events of the past few days. Molly had been through the emotional wringer—it was possible she wanted to unplug from the world for a while and recharge her batteries.

Max wanted to believe that, but his gut kept insisting something was wrong. So instead of joining Mason at the front door, he veered off through the kitchen.

"What are you doing?" Mason called, clearly exasperated.

"Just checking one last thing," Max replied. He reached the door that led to the garage and swung it open.

"Are you done yet? I don't want to be here when she gets home."

Max's stomach churned as he looked into the garage. "I don't think that's going to be a problem."

"How can you be sure?" Mason's voice was getting closer; he was apparently coming to check on Max.

Max stepped to the side so Molly's brother could see what he was looking at.

"Because her car is still here."

# Chapter 14

Molly shivered on the thin mattress, her body curled into a ball in a bid to conserve heat.

Her earlier assessment was correct—the thread-bare blanket Elaine had left her did little to keep her warm. She'd searched the other drawers of the file cabinet, hoping to find another blanket or even a towel, but had come up empty-handed.

It was shadowy in the office, though a dim gray light shone through the dusty glass panels set high into the walls of the warehouse proper. Molly wasn't wearing a watch, but if the light was anything to go by, the day was fading away into evening. She was already freezing—how was she going to survive the night, when the temperature dropped even further?

*I have to keep moving.* The thought propelled her

off the bed. She wrapped the blanket around herself like a cloak and began to pace the confines of the office, as much as her tether would allow. She'd already tested the strength of the chain, finding it frustratingly solid. She'd scoured every inch of the dirty floor for a discarded paper clip or stray staple, anything she could use to try to pick the lock of the handcuffs around her ankle. But she'd found nothing.

Now, as she walked, she tried not to let her mind wander. She'd learned earlier in the day that if she didn't control her thoughts she'd wind up thinking about Max, and that would make her cry. Her still-swollen nose couldn't handle any more tears, so Molly focused on her current situation, trying to come up with a way to break free from her prison cell.

Four steps forward, turn, four steps back. Over and over again. It wasn't much of a route, but the movement did make her feel a bit warmer.

Darkness fell as she walked. There had to be something she could use to get out of here, some tool she had overlooked in her initial panicked search. The desk was empty, but perhaps if she ripped one of the drawers free from its tracks she'd find a screw or a nail or something equally useful...

Something scuttered along the floor nearby. Molly's heart jumped into her throat, and she scrambled onto the bed. A soft squeak came from the corner of the office.

*Rats*, she realized. Probably here for the crumbs she'd dropped earlier when eating a granola bar.

Bile rose up the back of her throat. Molly swallowed hard, determined not to throw up. It was bad enough she'd already had to pee in the bucket by the desk. She wasn't going to make the situation even worse by vomiting all over herself.

She hugged her knees and began to rock, hoping the movement would help keep her warm. The bedsprings dug painfully into her flesh, making it hard to find a comfortable position. She shifted on the mattress, then gasped as inspiration struck.

The bedsprings! Maybe she could pry one free and use the end to pick the lock of the handcuffs!

A surge of adrenaline pushed her to her feet. She knelt by the bed, heedless of any rodents nearby. Feeling blindly in the dark, she shoved her hands under the mattress and encountered a wire mesh secured to the metal bed frame by several tight coils. If she could take it apart, she might be able to make a lock pick!

Something brushed her leg. She screamed, eliciting a startled squeak from her furry companions. Forgetting her mission, she jumped back onto the mattress. It wasn't comfortable, but it was a damn sight better than the floor.

It took a few minutes for her heart rate to return to normal. "Okay," she told herself. Somehow, the sound of her own voice made her feel less alone. "We obviously can't do this now. We'll just wait for the sun to come up, and then we can try again."

Her daughter shifted inside her, as if communicating her agreement with the plan.

"We've got this." Molly put her hand on her belly, patting softly. There were a million different reasons why this plan wouldn't work, but she refused to consider them now. Here in the cold darkness, she needed to focus on hope. It was the only way she would make it through the night.

Max and Mason stood on Molly's front porch, staring down the driveway in the fading light of the afternoon.

"I'm not sure we needed to call the police just yet," Mason said. "For one thing, we're not even certain she's missing."

Max didn't bother to look at the man. "She's not here. She's not answering her phone. Her car is still in the garage, and her purse is sitting on top of the washer. Where, pray tell, do you think she is?"

"Maybe she went for a walk?" Mason suggested weakly.

"No."

After finding Molly's car in the garage, Max had wasted no time calling the police. The dispatcher had told him help was on the way, but since it wasn't an emergency call, they weren't a high priority.

"Don't you have any family connections in law enforcement?" Max had asked after hanging up.

"Well, my cousin Trey is the sheriff…" Mason had said hesitantly.

"Call him."

"I'd hate to waste his time."

"Call. Him."

So Mason had made the call. Trey had promised to come. There was nothing to do now but wait.

And Max hated it.

His imagination ran wild, coming up with increasingly disturbing scenarios. What if Molly had taken a walk as Mason suggested, but been mauled by a bear or a mountain lion? What if she was lying in a ditch, bleeding and in pain? How would they ever find her?

His thoughts were interrupted by the appearance of a car. The vehicle turned into Molly's driveway, then stopped abruptly as the driver caught sight of Mason's truck and the two of them on the porch.

Max squinted in the gloam. "Is that the sheriff?"

"No." Mason leaned forward. "I think that's Elaine's car."

"Who's Elaine?"

"My wife." Mason waved at the driver. The car started forward again, pulling in behind Mason's truck. After a moment, the engine turned off and the driver's door opened.

Mason headed down the porch steps. "Hey, baby," he said to the blonde woman who emerged from the car. "What's going on?"

"Ah, nothing. What are you doing here?"

"We're looking for Molly." Mason and Elaine walked to the porch. She noticed Max, gave him a nod. He nodded back, studying her.

She seemed nervous, shifting her weight from foot to foot as she stood in place. Her eyes darted around, landing on him, then Furbert, then Mason, then the front door.

"Where is Molly?" she asked.

"We don't know," Max said before Mason had a chance to speak. "Have you seen or heard from her today?"

"Me?" She huffed out a laugh that sounded forced. "No. I'm the last person she'd want to talk to."

"Oh? Why's that?"

Elaine ducked her head. "We got into an argument the other day."

"You did?" Mason stared at his wife in surprise.

She nodded. "I said some unkind things to her after finding out about the baby."

Understanding flashed across Mason's face, and he pulled her close for a hug. "She knows you didn't mean them," he said.

Elaine closed her eyes. "That's why I'm here," she explained once Mason had released her. "I wanted to apologize."

Max tilted his head to the side as he watched her. There was something about this woman that didn't add up, though Mason didn't seem to think anything was wrong. But who showed up unannounced at dusk to apologize?

Another car turned onto the driveway. This driver pulled confidently forward, and in under a minute, a tall, broad-shouldered man walked toward them. "Mason. Elaine." He nodded at each one in turn. Then he looked at Max. "Trey Colton," he said, extending his hand.

Max shook it. "Max Hollick."

Recognition flashed across Trey's face. "I know

you by reputation," he said. "Your charity does good work."

"Thank you," Max replied reflexively. "I appreciate you coming out this evening."

"No problem. Now who wants to tell me what's going on? Mason, you said you're worried about your sister?"

Mason opened his mouth, but Max jumped in first. "I'm the reason he called." He explained his connection to Molly, then listed his concerns, including the fact that her car was still in the garage and her purse in the house. "She's pregnant," he finished. "I just want to know that she and the baby are fine."

Trey nodded, taking it all in with a quiet competence that made Max feel a little better. "Let's walk through her house," Trey suggested.

At his suggestion, they all traipsed inside. Max, Mason and Elaine stood in the living room while Trey explored the home, quietly moving from room to room.

Elaine continued to fidget as Trey searched. Even Mason noticed; he put his hand on her arm. "Everything okay?" he asked.

She nodded. "I'm just worried about Molly. I can't imagine where she'd go."

Max said nothing. He didn't trust himself to speak around Molly's brother and sister-in-law. It seemed that Mason was in denial about Molly's absence. Perhaps that was how the man coped with stress. That was fine for him, but Max wasn't about to sit around and twiddle his thumbs while he hoped for Molly's safe return.

After a few minutes, Trey joined them in the living room. "I see no signs of foul play," he said, confirming what Max had already observed.

"She didn't just disappear," Max insisted.

"Probably not," Trey said. "But I'm afraid it's too early to file a missing persons report."

"What can we do in the meantime?" Max wasn't about to passively wait out the clock. He'd organize a search party himself if it came to that.

"I'll alert my team, tell everyone to be on the lookout for Molly. Maybe someone will find her walking through town or headed home. I'm afraid that's all I can do for now."

Max bit his tongue. "I see," he said shortly.

Trey looked at each one of them. "I know you're all worried. This is out of character for Molly. But given the shocking news we've all had recently..." He trailed off, shook his head. "I'm hoping she just wanted some time to think and clear her mind."

"I'm sure that's it," Mason said, looking relieved at his cousin's suggestion.

"Yes," Elaine echoed weakly. "That must be it."

Max narrowed his eyes at the two of them, but didn't respond. "All right," he said, knowing it was futile to argue. "I suppose we'll just have to wait."

Trey nodded. "I'll check in first thing tomorrow morning. In the meantime, let me know if any of you hear from her."

"We will," Mason promised.

Trey headed for the door. "Mason, can I trust you to lock up here?"

"Yes," Mason replied. "Sorry to have bothered you."

"It's not a bother," Trey repeated. "Hopefully Molly will turn up soon, wondering what all the fuss is about." With a nod at Max, Trey walked out of Molly's house.

Max waited until he heard the man's car start. Then he turned to Elaine. "Can you give me a ride back to The Lodge?"

She flinched. "Um, surely it would be better if Mason—"

"I can't," Mason replied. "I've got to head back to the office, close up some things before going home. It won't take you long, sweetie."

"All right." She swallowed, pasted on a false smile. "I suppose it's not a problem."

"Thanks," Max said flatly. He followed her out to the car, Furbert trotting after him.

"Oh," she said, drawing up short. "Your dog."

"Don't worry," Max replied matter-of-factly. "He won't mess up your seats." He moved past Elaine and opened the back door of her sedan. Furbert hopped inside, arranging himself on the seat. Then Max opened the passenger door, pausing for a second as he caught sight of a small dark spot on the upholstery.

*Is that blood?*

He couldn't go in for a closer look, not without arousing suspicion. So he climbed into the car, shutting the door after him. When Elaine opened her door, the courtesy lights inside the car flashed on again. Max took advantage of the momentary illumination to examine the headrest of his seat as he turned and grabbed the seat belt. There, clinging to the fabric, was a single golden strand of hair.

A chill went through him at the sight. Elaine had blond hair, but Max knew in his bones this strand belonged to Molly.

He forced himself to buckle the seat belt as if nothing was wrong. But inside, his mind was churning.

Elaine had taken Molly—he knew that much, even though his conclusion would never stand up in a court of law. But why would Mason's wife do that? She'd mentioned having an argument with Molly earlier. What had they fought about?

What had driven this woman to kidnap Molly? More importantly, what had she done with her?

Was Molly already dead? Had Elaine come back to her house to get rid of any evidence she'd left behind? Maybe so, but neither he nor Mason nor Trey had noticed anything unusual. If Elaine had killed Molly, she would have had to do it elsewhere.

Why go back to the house at all, then? She'd clearly been coming for something. But whatever the reason, she'd had to change her plans upon catching sight of Max and Mason.

He didn't for one minute believe her line about coming to apologize to Molly. And while her hesitation upon first seeing her husband and Max could be read as surprise, he knew in his gut it was shock that had made her pause. She'd had to come up with a lie on the spot to explain her presence, and while she may have fooled Mason, Max wasn't so easily convinced.

What should he do now? He wanted to grab the woman by the shoulders and shake the truth out of her. His fingertips itched with the urge to do violence, to extract a confession from her by any means necessary. If this woman had killed Molly... He released the thought, knowing that if he followed it to its conclusion, he'd lose the tenuous grip he had on his self-control.

*She's not dead*, he told himself. She couldn't be. He wouldn't allow it, and that was that.

He slid a glance at Elaine as she drove. Should he prod her a bit, see if she revealed anything? Or would she panic if he got too close to the truth? Only one way to find out...

"Where do you think Molly is?"

Elaine jumped at the sound of his voice, though he'd spoken quietly. "Oh! Ah, I'm sure she's just taking a little time for herself." A trill of a laugh escaped her, the sound more suited to a garden party than a serious conversation.

"I hope you're right," he said sincerely.

"Honestly, you shouldn't worry," Elaine said. "Besides, I hear through the grapevine you're leaving soon? Maybe Molly is simply lying low until you're gone."

"Or maybe she's avoiding you," he suggested. "After all, you're the one who fought with her the other day."

Elaine didn't respond, but he thought he saw a flash of emotion cross her face.

"What did you argue about, anyway?"

"You wouldn't understand." But Max could tell by the set of her mouth she wanted to say more. So he remained silent, hoping she'd continue to talk.

She didn't disappoint. "You're the baby's father, right?"

He nodded.

"Well, you should know Molly isn't taking proper care of herself."

"How's that?"

"She's drinking coffee. You're not supposed to have caffeine during pregnancy. And when I was there the other day, I saw beer in her fridge."

Max had noticed that the other night, too, but he wasn't worried. The evidence Elaine found so damning was nothing more than a treat Molly had bought for him during his last visit almost six months ago.

"You think she's drinking alcohol?"

Elaine shrugged. "All I know is that if that was my baby—" She broke off, pursing her lips.

Her words made the hair on the back of Max's neck stand at attention. Was Elaine jealous of the pregnancy? Had she taken Molly as part of some kind of bizarre "intervention" she'd deluded herself into thinking was necessary?

Before he could think of another question, she pulled into the round drive in front of The Lodge. "Here you are," she announced, relief evident in her voice.

Max climbed out of the car and opened the door for Furbert. "Thanks for the ride," he said evenly. He held the passenger door open so she couldn't take off. "I hope you and Mason will let me know if you hear from Molly."

"Naturally. But as I said before, I wouldn't worry. I'm sure she's fine."

Max closed the door and watched as Elaine sped away like her hair was on fire. Her nervous demeanor, her words regarding Molly's behavior, the possible blood spot on her car's seat and the blond hair clinging to the passenger headrest—it all pointed to Elaine's involvement in Molly's disappearance.

"Three strikes," he muttered to himself. In the service, he'd had a simple philosophy—there's no such thing as a coincidence. So the fact that Molly's sister-in-law just happened to have a suspicious-looking spot and blond hair in her car on the same day Molly went missing? It was as good as a confession to him.

So what now? The sheriff wasn't likely to act on the basis of Max's suspicions. He seemed like a good man, but one who followed the rules. Max didn't have time for "by the book," not when Molly's life and that of his unborn daughter were at stake.

Maybe it was time to dust off some of his old covert skills...

Max walked into the lobby of The Lodge and marched up to the concierge desk, Furbert on his heels.

"I need to rent a car."

# Chapter 15

Molly came awake with a jolt, her eyes flying open and her heart thumping hard against her ribs.

She glanced around the room. Rusted desk, dilapidated file cabinet, thin blanket—yep, all still there.

She wasn't aware of having fallen asleep—hadn't meant to, in fact. But sometime during the night, fatigue had gotten the best of her.

Her body ached, a combination of the chilly air and her uncomfortable quarters. Her muscles were so stiff she felt as though she were sporting a full-body cast. God, would she even be able to move—?

Only one way to find out. Slowly, carefully, she pushed herself into a sitting position. After a few steadying breaths, she placed her feet on the floor and stood up. A moan escaped her as her legs protested her weight. The sound echoed in the empty, cavernous warehouse, startling a nesting bird in the rafters. It took off with an indignant chirp, feathers rustling as it flew. Molly watched the bird escape through one of the broken windows set high in the wall, wishing she could scale those heights herself.

She squinted at the window, trying to gauge the time. The light was thin and watery, a pale illumination that did little more than allow Molly to see her hand in front of her face. But it was better than the total darkness of last night.

Her stomach growled and her throat cried out for water. Molly shuffled over to the file cabinet, the chain at her ankle clanging as she moved. She grabbed a granola bar and a bottle of water and returned to the bed, lowering herself onto the mattress with a grunt.

She chewed without tasting, eating only to keep up her strength. When she was done, she put the trash in one of the empty desk drawers. After availing herself of the bucket, she stood in front of the bed, eyeing it with a frown.

The light was stronger now, which made things easier. Molly lifted the mattress, getting her first good look at the wire mesh underneath. Thin metal wire was laid out in a grid pattern, with each strip anchored to the bed frame by a tightly coiled metal spring. If she could pry one of the springs free, she could expose the end of one of the wires. It looked small enough to fit in the lock of the handcuffs at her ankle, and since she had nothing but time on her hands, she should eventually be able to release the lock.

Molly knelt next to the bed, ignoring the ache in her thighs and knees. She grabbed the closest spring and gave it an experimental tug. Rust flaked off into her hand and rained onto the floor with a soft patter. The metal of the spring was rough, and it scratched her hands as she pulled and shoved and pried, trying to move it from its spot. Her fingers and palms began to sting as rust and grime came into contact with the lacerations. Hissing through her teeth, Molly continued her efforts until her hands were slick with blood.

She wiped them across the front of her shirt and attacked the spring again. Now that her skin was dry she was able to get a better grip on the metal. Her arms began to ache as she continued to pull, but gradually the spring began to move, rewarding her for her efforts.

Excitement thrummed through her as she worked one end of the spring free from the tiny hole in the bed frame. "Come on," she muttered. Her fingers slipped, losing purchase. The spring slid out of her grasp, falling back into place. Molly cursed a blue streak, but dried her hands on her shirt and started again. Now that she knew she could move it, she was determined to keep at it until the spring was free.

After several minutes of effort, the spring slid out of its berth with a metallic scratch. Molly let out a triumphant yell and rocked back on her heels. She'd done it!

Now that the spring was no longer under tension, it was easy work to unhook it from the metal wire that made up the grid. Molly soon held the free end of the wire in her hand, ready to use.

She tried to bring her ankle close, but the angle was too awkward. Thinking fast, Molly put the mattress back onto the bed and climbed on top. From that angle, she was able to tug one side of the mattress up so she had access to the wire. She sat with her legs folded crisscross style, putting the handcuff around her ankle in close proximity to the wire. The wire wasn't very long, so she still had to contort herself a bit, but she was able to insert the thin metal end into the lock of the cuffs.

She grinned, feeling a flicker of hope for the first time since Elaine had abducted her.

"We're on our way, baby," she said, pushing her hair out of her face so she could focus on the task at hand. "I'm going to get us out of here."

Max shifted in the front seat of his rental car, trying to find a more comfortable position. It was chilly in the car, but he and Furbert had huddled together under a blanket most of the night, so he was actually pretty comfortable. Certainly warmer than he'd been during many nights on patrol in the desert.

Could Molly say the same? Was she inside somewhere, out of the elements? Or had Elaine staked her to a tree in the woods without a backward glance? And just what was driving this woman anyway? Why target Molly, who was one of the kindest people he'd ever met? Was she really that upset over Molly's perceived pregnancy infractions?

*Please let her be safe.*

It was the concern that had dominated his thoughts all night. After Elaine's shady actions, Max had decided he couldn't risk letting her out of his sight for long. She was connected to Molly's disappearance, and it was only a matter of time before she slipped up and gave herself away.

Hopefully sooner rather than later.

The concierge had pulled a few strings to get the rental car, and Max had wasted no time driving to Mason and Elaine's house, stopping only for a few provisions. He'd parked down the street and settled in to watch, knowing in his gut that Elaine was up to something.

There was a desperation about her, a brittleness that made him think she was about to snap. Mason didn't seem to recognize his wife's facade; Max had the impression Mason spent more time at work than he did with Elaine. So either he wasn't around enough to see his wife was troubled, or he threw himself into his job so he didn't have to deal with the problem. Regardless, Mason clearly wasn't going to be any help.

That was fine. Max was more than capable of operating alone.

He'd briefly considered calling Blaine, but didn't want to bother his friend. Furthermore, he didn't want to put Blaine in the position of having to act against one of his cousins. Better for Max to tackle this solo. He could always call for help if it came to that.

So he'd sat in the car, watching and waiting through the night for Elaine to make her move. She was spooked. Unless Max missed his guess, Elaine hadn't thought anyone would notice Molly's absence so soon. She was likely panicking, rethinking what she'd done.

Hopefully it wasn't anything permanent.

In the small hours of the night, Max had forced himself to once again consider the possibility Molly was dead. It had made him physically ill to even think about a world without Molly in it, but he wanted to be emotionally prepared in case the worst had happened.

His reaction had forced him to rethink his position on things. Once upon a time, he'd known how precious life was. How precarious it could be, and that he couldn't count on tomorrow. The service had taught him that things weren't always in his control, and he shouldn't take anything for granted. But somewhere along the way, he'd forgotten that lesson. He'd been too afraid to take the leap with Molly because he'd let his fears dictate his thinking. And the worst part? He'd lost sight of the truly important things in life—family, friends, love.

Max knew better now.

He would always be proud of K-9 Cadets. But it would no longer be his life's focus. Now that he was faced with the possibility of losing Molly forever, his earlier worries about commitment faded into nothingness. There were definitely things he needed to work on, and the path they walked together wouldn't always be smooth. But an imperfect life with Molly was far better than a perfect life without her.

If she'd still have him.

The only thing that worried him as much as Molly's uncertain fate was the thought that he'd irreparably damaged his chances with her. She'd opened her heart to him the other day, laying bare her hopes for their baby and their future. And he'd shut her down, making it clear he didn't think they had what it took to go the distance. He'd give anything to be able to go back in time and swallow those words, to stop himself from causing her so much pain.

He marveled at her response as he replayed the memories of their conversation. Even after breaking her heart, Molly had said she was still amenable to letting him see their baby. Her willingness to continue to be around him for the sake of their child was yet another sign of her selflessness and kindness. She was far better than he deserved, and he was going to spend the rest of his life trying to make her see that he knew how special she was.

Furbert nudged Max's leg, interrupting his thoughts. "Need a bathroom break, buddy?" The dog gazed up at him with knowing brown eyes, and Max reached out to scratch behind one of his ears. "Good idea. Let's stretch our legs a bit."

He climbed out of the car and led the dog to the end of the street, away from Mason and Elaine's house. It was growing lighter by the minute, and their neighbors were already starting to leave for work. If anyone noticed them, Max wanted it to look like he and his dog were out for a walk, nothing more.

While Furbert did his business, Max kept an eye on the house. He heard the rumble of a truck's engine from somewhere nearby. A few seconds later, Mason's truck backed out of the driveway and headed down the street.

Max glanced at Furbert, who was now sniffing at another patch of grass. "Come on," he said, giving the leash a gentle tug to get the dog's attention. He felt bad that he hadn't been able to give his friend a longer break outside the car, but now that Mason had left for work, Max was willing to bet Elaine would make her move soon.

Sure enough, his instincts were proven correct when she pulled out of the driveway a few minutes later.

"Bingo," he whispered. He felt the adrenaline hit his system as he turned the key in the ignition. Thanks to his years of experience, the hormone surge didn't make him jittery. Rather, a sense of calm descended over him, his senses hyper-focused and attuned to his environment.

He waited about a minute after Elaine had left before pulling into the road behind her. It was possible she was simply going to the grocery store or headed to the gym. If that was the case, he and Furbert were in for a long, boring day.

But Max didn't care. He'd follow her around forever, because he knew in his bones that at some point, she'd lead him to the woman he loved.

## Chapter 16

Molly swore as the wire slipped out of the lock once more, skittering across the smooth surface of the cuffs. Picking the lock was proving to be more difficult than she'd anticipated. She was able to fit the wire into the lock opening, but it seemed no matter how she rotated or jiggled or pushed it, she couldn't find the right angle to release the catch.

Her frustration was at its peak, but she refused to give up. There was no telling when—or even if—Elaine would be coming back. Molly wasn't going to sit around waiting for fate to catch up with her. She owed it to herself and her baby to keep trying.

Her fingers were still stiff, though now it was due to clutching the wire rather than the cold. It was growing steadily brighter inside the warehouse;

morning was well under way by now. Molly wasn't sure how long she'd been working, but it didn't matter. She was determined to continue until she was either free or dead.

Obviously, she was hoping for the former outcome.

She released her grip on the wire, bending and straightening her fingers to release some of the tension. A short break wouldn't hurt, and might even help if it restored some of her manual dexterity.

Max's face flashed through her mind. With his Special Forces training, he'd know just how to get out of these handcuffs. Of course, he probably wouldn't have let himself be taken in the first place, gun notwithstanding.

She closed her eyes, imagining he was with her now.

*Don't give up*, he'd say. *You're doing great.*

He'd been so calm during their time in the gondola. Had it really only been a few days since the avalanche? With everything that had happened, it felt like a lifetime ago.

Her mind drifted, remembering the solid feel of his body against hers as she'd leaned on him. The way it had felt to wake up in his arms, pretending for a few seconds that nothing had changed between them. She'd love to be able to go back to that afternoon, when she was still ignorant of her sister's murder and Max hadn't definitively broken her heart yet. Sure, she'd been hanging precariously in a glass carriage, risking death with each gust of wind. But compared to her current situation, that seemed like a cakewalk.

All because of Max's presence.

It was amazing how his company made her feel better. From swinging in the gondola to her sister's murder, having Max by her side made her feel grounded, like she could handle anything.

But he wasn't here now. And he'd made it clear he didn't want to be her rock, didn't want to walk through life by her side. So she was going to have to figure out a way to take care of things on her own.

The thought galvanized her into action once more. She examined the end of the wire, used her thumbnail to bend it just a smidge. Then she inserted it into the lock, feeling blindly for the latch that would set her free.

A little to the left... No, up a bit... A hair to the right...

The wire suddenly sank in a bit. Molly's heart jumped into her throat and she took a deep breath, trying to hold her hands steady so they didn't jerk the wire free.

Working carefully, she prodded here, poked there. One little twist, and then...

The cuff around her ankle slid open, releasing her. Molly jerked her leg away with a sob, and the cuffs and chain slid off the mattress to clatter on the floor.

Molly got to her feet, tears blurring her vision. Relief made her feel light-headed, so she sat on the bed once more to collect herself.

Her chest heaved as she gulped air, trying to organize her thoughts. She'd get out of here, follow the road until she found someone, anyone to help her. As soon as she made it back to Roaring Springs, she was headed straight for the sheriff's office.

A noise at the far end of the warehouse caught her attention. The door opened, and in walked Elaine, carrying a paper bag.

Molly's mind raced as she considered her options. She could run now, try to make her escape while Elaine had her hands full. Or she could pretend to still be restrained and wait for the other woman to leave. That was the safer choice, especially if Elaine had brought her gun again.

But if Molly could overpower her sister-in-law, she could grab her keys and use her car to escape. After the long, cold night Molly wasn't in the best shape to attempt a walk back into town. The only abandoned warehouses Molly knew about sat a few miles outside Roaring Springs, a bit off the main road. If that was indeed where she was, having the car would definitely make life easier.

Elaine was getting closer; she had to make a decision.

Molly bent forward and snagged the open end of the handcuffs. She bent her leg at the knee, tucking her ankle under her opposite thigh. Then she stuck the chain under her ankle, to make it look like she was still attached. She leaned back against the wall, forcing herself to sit still while Elaine approached.

"Good morning!" Elaine sounded chipper. "I

brought you a few more supplies." She set the paper bag on the desk and began unpacking it.

"How was your night?"

"Cold," Molly said shortly. How was she going to do this? Positionally, she was at a disadvantage. It would take a few seconds for her to stand up, plenty of time for Elaine to go on the defensive. Maybe she could use the chain as a whip, lashing out at Elaine before she could react? She stroked the cold links with her fingertip, considering the possibility.

"This should help," Elaine said. She pulled out a metal thermos and handed it to Molly. "Hot tea."

Molly smiled, unable to believe her luck. "Thank you," she said.

"Of course," Elaine replied. "As I told you before, I want you to stay healthy." She turned back to the bag, reaching in for more items.

Molly hefted the thermos in her hands. It was a nice, heavy weight, and with a handle on the side to boot. Exactly what she needed.

Elaine continued to chatter as she pulled items from the bag and placed them on the desk surface. While she talked, Molly slowly rose from the bed and moved to stand behind the other woman.

"I brought you another blanket…" Elaine trailed off as she turned and realized Molly was no longer sitting on the bed. She looked to the side, just in time to meet Molly's eyes as Molly brought the thermos crashing down onto her head.

Elaine collapsed in a heap on the floor. Molly dropped the thermos and ran, not bothering to check if the other woman was still alive. She rushed through the empty warehouse, fearing that at any second Elaine would rise up and shoot her in the back.

The shot never came. Molly burst through the door, throwing up her arm to shield her eyes from the bright sunlight.

She was free.

Max trailed behind Elaine's car, keeping his distance so as not to draw her attention. She drove through town, headed for the outskirts. He had to back off a bit as traffic thinned out, but it was easy enough to keep her in sight.

A few miles outside Roaring Springs she turned on a side road. Max slowed down, then did the same, hanging back to let her get ahead. He needn't have worried. Elaine sped forward, oblivious to her surroundings. She pulled into the parking lot of what looked like an abandoned warehouse. Max stopped his car about a hundred yards away, partially shielded by a clump of bushes. As he watched, Elaine pulled a paper bag from the passenger seat of her car and entered the warehouse.

*Supplies?* he wondered. Food, perhaps? Maybe toiletries? Whatever it was, Elaine clearly hadn't come to set up a garden party.

Max waited, imagining her progress through the warehouse. He didn't want to spook her too soon, or she might hurt Molly.

Convinced she was too far into the building to

hear the engine of his car, he pulled in beside her, putting the passenger door of his rental only inches from her driver's door. If she tried to escape, she wouldn't be able to get behind the wheel easily. Hopefully it was a precaution he didn't need to take, but Max knew from experience that in an operation, every second counted.

He climbed out of his car, leaving the door open so she wouldn't hear it shut. Then he approached the building carefully, his gaze assessing as he studied the structure. The door Elaine had used appeared to be the only entrance on this side. What about the back of the building? Was there another entry point he could use to take her by surprise?

Max started for the nearest corner, intending to scout the perimeter. His emotions urged him to run inside, to chase down Elaine before she could do anything to Molly. But his training wouldn't allow him to rush into a scene without more information. If Molly was in there, his best chance of helping her depended upon him keeping his cool.

He'd made it only a few steps when the door Elaine had just used burst open with a sound like a shot. A figure stumbled out, blond hair flying as she ran.

Molly!

She threw up her arm to shield her eyes from the sun. Max took a step toward her. "Molly!" he cried.

She flinched at the sound of his voice. Without looking at him, she pivoted away from him and tried to run.

Max caught up to her easily, wrapping his arms around her to keep her from falling on the uneven ground.

Molly fought like a wild thing, bucking and twisting and scratching at his hands and arms. "Let me go!" she yelled.

"Molly, it's me! It's Max!" He tightened his grip, applying just enough pressure to keep hold of her without hurting her. "It's Max!"

She stilled in his arms. "Max?" Her voice sounded small, but oh so hopeful.

"Yes," he said, trembling a bit as emotions threatened to overwhelm him. "I'm here, Molly. I'm here."

She turned around, blinking as she stared up at his face. When she met his eyes, she burst into tears.

He held her close as she sobbed against his chest, keeping one eye on the door in case Elaine should emerge.

"What happened?" He pulled back enough to get a good look at her. Her hair was a tangled mess, her face pale and tear-streaked. But it was the sight of her shirt that made his heart skip a beat.

Dried blood smeared the front of her belly, horrifyingly dark against the white fabric.

"Where are you hurt?" He fumbled with the hem of her shirt, trying to pull it over her belly. "Is the baby okay?"

"I'm okay," she said. "It's from my hands."

She held them up so he could see her palms. Her skin was crisscrossed with dozens of shallow scratches, most crusted over with scabs but some still oozing blood.

Relief flooded Max, and he pulled her against him once more. She was fine. The baby was fine.

He could have stayed like that forever, holding her close, reveling in the fact that she was whole and alive and *here*. But he couldn't fully relax until he knew there was no longer a threat to Molly.

"Where's Elaine?"

Molly shuddered. "Inside the office. I hit her on the head with a thermos and ran after she collapsed. I'm not even sure if she's alive."

"I'll find out."

"No!" She tightened her grip on him. "Please don't leave me."

"I have to check," he said softly. "But you won't be alone."

He led her over to his car and opened the door to the back seat. Furbert let out a happy yip at the sight of Molly. She climbed inside the car and threw her arms around the dog.

Max withdrew his cell phone and handed it to her. "Do you know where we are?"

She nodded. "Good. Call the sheriff and tell him. Have them send an ambulance—no, make that two ambulances." No way was he going to ask Molly to share a rig with Elaine.

She nodded again, her blue eyes impossibly wide. "Please be careful," she whispered. "She might have a gun. That's how she forced me to go with her. I couldn't risk her hurting the baby..." Molly trailed off, tears filling her eyes.

Max knelt and cupped her cheek with one hand. "You don't ever have to explain your actions to me. I know you did what was best for you and the baby."

"I tried to," she said, sniffling with a wince.

"You did," he replied firmly. "Don't ever doubt it."

He gave her hand a squeeze, then released it. As he walked away from Molly, he tamped down his emotions and tried to get his head back in the game. Until he knew what had happened to Elaine, he couldn't fully relax.

He yanked open the door of the warehouse but didn't enter yet, waiting a second to see if Elaine was going to fire on him.

Nothing.

Cautiously, Max knelt and peeked around the corner, scanning the space before leaning out again.

From what he could see, the warehouse was abandoned. There were a few wire shelves set up along the far wall, but nothing that would provide cover. The office was situated at the opposite end of the building, a plate-glass window separating the space from the warehouse proper. Presumably, Elaine was in there.

Max made a quick trip back to the rental car.

"Is she dead?" Molly asked tearfully.

"I don't know yet," Max said. "I can't see her from here." He popped the trunk, grabbed the tire iron inside. It was a poor defense against a gun, but he felt better having a weapon to hand.

After another quick look to make sure the coast was clear, he entered the warehouse. Moving fast and staying low, he crept along the wall toward the office.

He crouched below the window, inching toward the door. Pressing his back to the wall, he listened hard, straining to hear any sounds from within.

Elaine was still inside—he could hear her breathing. *Not dead, then.* He felt a small spurt of satisfaction at the realization; after what she had done to Molly, Max wanted the woman to enjoy a long stint in prison.

He risked a glance into the room. She was sprawled on the floor, apparently unconscious. Max knew better than to assume, though. He hadn't come this far to get shot by a woman playing possum.

She didn't move when he entered the office. He knelt next to her, spying a large, bloody gash on her forehead and a dented green thermos on the floor nearby. *Way to go,* he thought, feeling a burst of pride at the evidence of Molly's handiwork.

A quick pat down turned up a small pistol in Elaine's front jacket pocket. A chill went down Max's spine as he imagined a different outcome for this fight, one in which Elaine had managed to grab her gun before Molly had clocked her across the head. A few seconds of hesitation, and he might be standing over Molly's lifeless body instead of Elaine's unconscious form.

Max glanced around the room, his anger building as he took in the surroundings: a rusted-out metal desk and file cabinet, a hospital bed that looked straight out of a horror flick, and a thick metal chain anchored to the middle of the floor.

But it was the plastic bucket by the desk that nearly pushed him over the edge.

"Damn you," he muttered.

Elaine began to stir, moaning softly. Not trusting himself to remain civilized, Max grabbed the handcuffs dangling from the end of the metal chain. He snapped the open end around Elaine's wrist, tightening the bracelet until it was flush against her skin so that she had no chance of sliding free.

"Let's see how you like it," he growled.

Sirens wailed in the distance, the high-pitched sound music to his ears. Hopefully the sheriff and ambulances would arrive soon. Molly looked superficially fine, but he wouldn't rest easy until she and the baby had been checked by a doctor.

Max stood and walked out of the office, leaving Elaine alone on the filthy floor. He paused just outside the warehouse, bending at the waist to set her gun on the ground in plain sight. Then he headed for the rental car, back to his woman and his baby and his dog.

His future.

# Chapter 17

"Back so soon?" Dr. Fitzpatrick tutted as he walked into Molly's room. "Don't take this the wrong way, but I had hoped not to see you again."

Molly smiled, appreciating the man's lighthearted tone. "I feel the same way. The last few days have been…challenging."

His lips pressed together as he nodded. "So I heard. I'm so sorry you went through that." He gave her foot a soft pat. "I'm glad you're okay."

"Me, too." She blinked, determined not to cry. She'd shed enough tears recently to last a lifetime.

"I peeked at your chart before coming in," Dr. Fitzpatrick said as he began flipping switches and turning dials on the ultrasound machine. "From what I saw, you're doing fine. A little dehydrated, but that's why they have you hooked up to this." He gestured to the IV line running saline into her arm. "We'll take a quick peek at the baby to confirm she's okay, too, and then send you on your way."

"That sounds nice," Molly replied. She wanted nothing more than to go home, crawl into her comfortable bed and sleep until the baby was due.

"I saw your husband in the waiting area, talking to the sheriff. Would you like me to wait for him to finish before I start the scan?"

Molly didn't bother to correct the doctor's misapprehension. "Ah, no. That's all right. I'm not sure how long he'll be tied up." It was the truth, but she still felt a twinge of guilt for proceeding in Max's absence. He probably would have liked to see the baby again.

"Fair enough," Dr. Fitzpatrick said. "Here comes the goo."

Less than a minute later, her daughter was on the screen. Molly watched as the baby kicked and rolled, seemingly unaware of the troubles going on in the wider world.

"Just as I thought," the doctor said as he moved the wand over her belly. "She's looking good."

He finished up and handed Molly a small towel with a smile. "Nothing to worry about here, mama. Your baby is doing just fine."

"That's good to know." A sense of relief washed over her, carrying away her last lingering worries. Now that she knew her baby was all right, she could truly relax.

Dr. Fitzpatrick pushed the cart toward the door. "Get some rest," he advised. "You've been through a lot. You need time to heal, and not just physically."

Molly nodded, a lump in her throat. "Thank you," she croaked.

He gave her a parting smile and left, unaware of how right he was.

Molly's body was fine. Sure, she had a few bumps and bruises, but nothing a hot bath and a good night's sleep couldn't help. No, the part of her that was truly broken was her heart.

First Sabrina. Then Max. The hits had come fast and hard, with no time for her to recover before suffering the next blow. What she needed more than anything was to retreat from the world so she could work on stitching her heart back together. Her baby deserved a happy, healthy mother, not a broken shell of the person she'd once been.

A soft knock sounded on the door. Max poked his head into the room. "Mind if I come in?"

*Speak of the devil*, she thought. She nodded her permission. He walked over to the side of the bed and looked down at her, his green eyes warm.

"Everything okay?" he asked. "I thought I saw the OB leave."

"You did," she confirmed. "He did a quick scan to make sure the baby is okay. He said everything looks good."

"I'm glad to hear it." He let out a sigh.

"How did your interview with Trey go?"

Max nodded. "I think it went well. I just told him

what I knew, what I'd done." Something about the set of Max's mouth made Molly think that wasn't all they'd discussed, but she didn't press the issue.

"And what did you know? You never told me how you found me." Now that the immediate shock of her ordeal was over, she was curious to know exactly how Max had been in the right place at the right time.

"It's kind of a long story," he said. He pulled a chair closer and sat down. "It all started yesterday afternoon…"

Molly listened in amazement as he told her his side of things, from going to her house to following Elaine's car out to the warehouse. "Wow," she said, truly impressed. "I'm so glad you figured out something was off with Elaine. I wouldn't have known what to do after calling the sheriff's office. Thank you for not giving up."

He shrugged, blushing a little. "It gave me an excuse to dust off my skills," he said, deflecting her gratitude.

"I'm just glad you were there to play the hero."

"Oh, please," he said. "You didn't need me. You came tearing out of there before I had a chance to save you." He reached for her hand, holding it between his own. The corners of his mouth turned up. "It was a real blow to my ego, let me tell you."

Molly laughed, rolling her eyes. "You look like you survived."

"Just barely." His expression turned serious now. "After hearing Elaine's plan to take the baby and kill you…" He trailed off, shaking his head. "I don't ever want to come close to losing you again."

Molly didn't know what to say to that. She studied his face, noticing the dark circles under his eyes and his wrinkled clothes. He looked like a man who'd been through hell. In another time, she would have taken him into her arms and held him while he slept. But he didn't want that from her anymore.

"There's something I want to say to you, but I know this might not be the best time."

She frowned. "What's on your mind?"

He took a deep breath. "I made a mistake, Molly. Earlier, when we talked about our future. I told you I didn't think I could give you what you need, that we wouldn't work. But I realize now I was wrong."

It was exactly what she'd hoped to hear from him. Two days ago. Now? She wasn't so sure…

"And what caused this revelation?" It was a complete reversal of what he'd said earlier. Hard to believe he'd so thoroughly changed his mind in such a short period of time.

Max leaned forward, lifting her hand to brush his lips across the back of her knuckles. "When I thought you were…dead," he said, grimacing over the word, "it made me reevaluate my life. I know now that I was wrong to put my work before you, before us. You and the baby are the most important things in my life, and I want to be here for the two of you, to give you everything you need."

It sounded so beautiful, the realization of all her

hopes and dreams. So why couldn't she accept that what he was saying was true?

Max's eyes searched her face. "You don't look happy."

"I don't think I am," she replied.

He frowned. "But…I thought this was what you wanted."

Molly lifted one eyebrow. "It was. But when you put it like that, I have to wonder if you really mean it, or if you're just saying it because you think that's what I want to hear."

"Why would I do that?"

"That's the part I can't figure out," Molly said. She sighed. "I want to trust you, Max, I do. But I can't think straight right now. You broke my heart the other day." Tears welled in her eyes, and he looked away, guilt flashing across his face. "How do I know you're not going to do it again?"

"Molly, I won't—"

"You say that now," she interrupted. "But have your feelings really changed? Or is this just a knee-jerk reaction in the wake of Elaine's actions?"

"It's not," he said firmly. "It's more than that."

She shook her head. "Max, you said you couldn't commit to me because you're already so involved with your charity. That hasn't changed. So why do you suddenly think you can multitask, when before, you'd made up your mind that wasn't possible?"

"Don't you see? When we spoke before, I'd lost sight of what's most important to me. You and the baby."

"So you're ready to be a full-time dad now? No more monthly visitations?" Molly didn't bother to keep the edge from her tone.

Max winced. "Not my best idea, it's true. But to answer your question, yes. I do want to be here for the baby, from the beginning."

Molly absorbed his words, wishing she could let go of her hurt and doubts and trust everything he was saying. She could tell from the look in Max's eyes that he genuinely believed he was telling her the truth. But she wasn't ready to take the chance that he wouldn't change his mind once the shock of this experience wore off and real life set in again.

Max gave her a sad smile and got to his feet. "I can see you don't believe me. And that's my fault. But I'm serious—I want us to be together, to raise our daughter together as a family."

Molly said nothing. She held his gaze, wishing she could give him the answer he so clearly wanted.

"I'll leave you now. Blaine is here…he said he'd take you home. Again," he added with a soft laugh. He leaned in, pressed his lips to hers in an impossibly sweet kiss. "But we're not finished yet. I'm going to prove to you I meant every word I said here tonight."

"Max…" She shook her head, unable to see how he could do that.

"Don't worry," he said. "I know what I need to do. You just rest. Take care of our little one." He placed his hand on her belly, a large, warm weight against her skin. As if sensing her father's touch, the baby shifted and kicked.

Max's eyes widened. "Was that—?"

Molly couldn't help but smile. "Yes. That's her."

A delighted grin spread across his face. He leaned over, putting his mouth close to her belly. "Hello, Little Bit. I'm your daddy. I have to go now, but I'll be back soon." He paused a second, then added, "I love you."

Molly blinked away tears, touched by his heartfelt sentiment. He was normally so serious and reserved; it was nice to see him soften toward their daughter.

He straightened and met her gaze. "Call me when you're ready to see me again."

"Aren't you going back home on Friday?" They would have to figure out some kind of visitation schedule before he left. Molly knew if she waited until he was back at work, she'd be talking to his secretary instead of him.

"No." Max shook his head. "I've canceled my flight reservation."

His answer surprised her. "How long will you be staying in town?"

His green eyes sparkled with an emotion she couldn't name.

"Indefinitely."

"Are you sure you don't need anything, dear? The girls and I would be happy to cook for you, run errands or do laundry. Anything you need."

Molly held the phone to her ear and smiled on Friday morning. "I appreciate the offer, Aunt Mara. But I know you and Phoebe and Skye already have your hands full planning the film festival." Her cousins had both dropped by yesterday to check on her. She'd enjoyed seeing the twins, but could tell they were stressed to the max already. Phoebe was coordinating the awards ceremony for the festival, while Skye was focused on making all the arrangements for the movie stars who would be attending.

"But that's not all," Skye had said, practically vibrating with excitement. "I've been asked to cover the festival for an online magazine." She'd rattled off the name of the site, and Molly had pretended to recognize it. "They want me to do live interviews with the stars from several of the events! I can't wait!"

Molly had smiled, happy for her cousins. Their joy was a bright spot in her otherwise gray mood.

"We'll always make time for family," Aunt Mara said, pulling Molly back to the present conversation. "I know your parents are due to arrive today. Please call me when they get in. I want to see them."

"I will," Molly replied. She ended the call, then dialed Mason. He hadn't responded to her calls or texts yesterday, and she was worried about him.

"Hello?"

Relief filled her at the sound of her brother's voice, even though she could tell he was in a bad way. "Mason! I've been trying to reach you."

"I know."

"Are you okay?"

He sighed. "No. I'm not." He was silent, and for a second, Molly thought she heard him crying.

"Mason, please come over. Or let me come to you."

He sniffed. "I can't, Mols. Not right now."

"You know I don't blame you, right?" In the aftermath of her rescue, it had become abundantly clear that Elaine had acted alone. Mason hadn't had any idea of his wife's awful plan or of her actions. He'd been horrified to discover what she'd done, and he'd called Molly just as she was leaving the hospital, apologizing profusely for what had happened.

"I know," he replied. "But that doesn't mean I don't blame myself."

"Please don't," Molly said. "You're not responsible for what other people do."

"That's sweet of you to say…"

Molly heard a voice in the background that sounded like an intercom. "Where are you?"

"I'm at the airport," Mason said. "I need to get away for a while. Sort some things out."

She tightened her grip on the phone, alarmed at his words. She'd already lost her sister; was she going to lose her brother, as well? "Where are you headed?"

"Away," he said shortly.

"But…" She cast about for something to say, something to convince him to stay in town. He needed to be around family right now, to know that they all still loved and supported him. "What about your work on the film festival? You can't just leave Phoebe and Skye and Aunt Mara in the lurch!"

"I'm not. Seth is going to take over for me. I already told Phoebe."

Molly recognized the name—Seth was one of the managers at The Lodge. He seemed nice enough, but his inclusion at the last minute must have heightened Aunt Mara's stress level.

"What about Elaine? You're just going to leave her?"

"I'm not abandoning her," he said, an edge to his voice. "She's at the state psychiatric hospital, for crying out loud. They'll take care of her while I'm gone."

"I wish you wouldn't do this," Molly said. "Mom and Dad will be here today. Don't you want to see them?"

"I have to get away," Mason said softly. "My life is in shambles right now. I need to figure out how to put it back together."

"Okay," she said simply. "Just know that I love you, and I'll be here to help you when you're ready to come home."

"Thanks. I needed to hear that." He sighed. "I've got to go. They're boarding my flight."

"Have a safe trip."

"Thanks. Take care of yourself, Mols. And the baby, too."

He hung up before she could respond. Molly set the phone on the coffee table and remained on the couch, processing this latest development.

She closed her eyes, seeing Max's face. It would be nice to talk to him about Mason, tell him what was going on. He'd know just what to say to make her feel better, and Furbert would press himself against her side until she was so busy paying attention to him she'd forget to be worried.

Her hand hovered over the phone, but she pulled it back. She couldn't call up Max every time she was upset. She needed to find new ways of dealing with her feelings, so that when he went back to his old life she wasn't left out in the cold.

Searching for a distraction, she picked up the remote and turned on the television. Maybe there was something mindless on. She flipped through the channels, pausing when she saw Max's face.

*He's on the news*, she realized, leaning forward. But why?

A reporter was asking him questions about her abduction and his role in her rescue. "How do you know the victim, Molly Gilford?"

"Molly and I have been seeing each other for a little over two years now," Max said easily.

Molly blinked, surprised to hear him publicly acknowledge their relationship.

"And is it true you're expecting your first child together?"

"Yes, that's correct. I'm very excited about it."

Molly placed her hand on her belly, recalling the tender look on his face as he'd told their daughter he loved her.

The woman smiled. "I can imagine. You said earlier you're planning to move to Roaring Springs. Will you be able to manage your charity, K-9 Cadets, from here?"

"I'm not too worried about that," Max replied.

"You see, I'm stepping down as managing director of K-9 Cadets. I want to focus on Molly and our family, and while I love my work, it simply takes up too much time. I'll be staying on as a consultant, but the actual day-to-day job of running the organization will fall to my replacement."

The reporter made another remark, but Molly didn't hear what the woman said. She was too stunned by Max's announcement to pay attention to anything else.

He was resigning from K-9 Cadets? And moving here?

She shook her head, hardly daring to believe it. But he'd just confessed, on television, that he wanted to focus on their family.

It was a hell of a statement.

Suddenly, his voice echoed in her head. *I'm going to prove to you I meant every word I said here tonight.*

And so he had.

Max had rearranged his life to make sure he'd have time for her and the baby. He'd turned his world upside down, then done the equivalent of shouting the news from the rooftops. It was a big, bold, unmistakable gesture on his part. Not something he could easily reverse or undo. No, these changes were the kind that would stick.

Molly grabbed the phone, needing to hear his voice. To know this was real, not just some strange hallucination on her part.

He answered on the first ring. "Molly?"

"You said for me to call you when I was ready to see you again. I'm ready now."

She heard the gust of his breath over the line. "That's good," he said, chuckling softly. "Because I'm in your driveway."

"You are?" She walked to the front door and stepped onto the porch. Sure enough, Max's rental car was sitting in front of her house. "Are you going to come in?"

He climbed out of the car, followed by Furbert. He walked up to the porch steps, phone still at his ear. "I wasn't going to bother you. I was just coming to see the baby." He gave her a wink, then reached out, touching her belly gently with his free hand.

"She'll be happy to hear your voice again."

Max began to climb the stairs, stopping when they were at eye level. "I missed you," he whispered, shoving his phone into his pocket.

"I missed you, too," she admitted.

He leaned in to kiss her, but she held up her hand. "Is it true?"

"Is what true?"

"I just saw you on the news. You're really stepping down as managing director?"

He nodded. "I am. The search is on for my replacement."

She examined his face, looking for any hint of regret. But his soft green eyes held only warmth as he stared back at her.

"And you're moving here, too?"

Another nod. "That's the plan."

"Where are you going to live?"

He tilted his head to the side. "See, that's the thing. I was kind of hoping you could help me with that." A boyish grin spread across his face.

Molly couldn't help but smile in return. "I think I can do that. But I have some conditions."

"Oh? Name them." He leaned in, pressing his mouth to hers.

She indulged in the kiss for a moment, then pulled back. "Rule number one—always use a coaster."

Max kissed her again. "Okay," he said against her lips.

"Rule number two—put the toilet seat down when you're done."

He pulled her close, lifting his hand to trace the curve of her cheek. "I can do that."

Molly shivered as sparks of sensation raced down her limbs to settle low in her belly. "And rule number three—don't ever leave."

Max smiled as he wrapped his arms around her. "That won't be a problem, I promise you. I love you, Molly. I'm never letting you go again."

His words triggered a flood of joy in her chest. "I love you, too, Max." She pressed her forehead against his, sharing his breath. "I think in some way I always have."

"I do look my best when I'm fresh from the shower," he drawled.

Molly threw back her head and laughed. "Let's test that theory, shall we?" She took his hand and led him across the porch.

"I'll go wherever you want," Max said. "As long as you go with me."

Molly paused on the threshold. "You've got yourself a deal."

Max dipped his head and kissed her soundly. Then he took her hand and they stepped inside the house.

Together.

\* \* \* \* \*

# Get 4 FREE REWARDS!

## We'll send you 2 FREE Books <u>plus</u> 2 FREE Mystery Gifts.

**Harlequin® Romantic Suspense** books feature heart-racing sensuality and the promise of a sweeping romance set against the backdrop of suspense.

FREE Value Over $20

---

**YES!** Please send me 2 FREE Harlequin® Romantic Suspense novels and my 2 FREE gifts (gifts are worth about $10 retail). After receiving them, if I don't wish to receive any more books, I can return the shipping statement marked "cancel." If I don't cancel, I will receive 4 brand-new novels every month and be billed just $4.99 per book in the U.S. or $5.74 per book in Canada. That's a savings of at least 12% off the cover price! It's quite a bargain! Shipping and handling is just 50¢ per book in the U.S. and 75¢ per book in Canada.* I understand that accepting the 2 free books and gifts places me under no obligation to buy anything. I can always return a shipment and cancel at any time. The free books and gifts are mine to keep no matter what I decide..

240/340 HDN GMYZ

Name (please print)

Address                                                                 Apt. #

City                              State/Province                    Zip/Postal Code

### Mail to the Reader Service:
**IN U.S.A.:** P.O. Box 1341, Buffalo, NY 14240-8531
**IN CANADA:** P.O. Box 603, Fort Erie, Ontario L2A 5X3

*Want to try 2 free books from another series? Call 1-800-873-8635 or visit www.ReaderService.com.*

---

Rebel asked more seriously, "How should a woman be treated,
then?"

Avi smiled broadly. Now they were getting somewhere. "It
would be my pleasure to show you."

She leaned back, staring openly at him. He was tempted to dare
her to take him up on it. After all, no Special Forces operator he'd
ever known could turn down a dare. But he was probably better
served by backing off and letting her make the next move. Not to
mention she deserved the decency on his part.

Waiting out her response was harder than he'd expected it to be.
He wanted her to take him up on the offer more than he'd realized.

"What would showing me entail?" she finally asked.

He shrugged. "It would entail whatever you're comfortable
with. Decent men don't force women to do anything they don't
want to do or are uncomfortable with."

"Hmm."

Suppressing a smile at her hedging, he said quietly, "They do,
however, insist on yes or no answers to questions of whether they
should proceed. Consent must always be clearly given."

He waited her out while the SUV carrying Piper and Zane
pulled up at the gate to the Olympic Village.

Gunnar delivered them to the back door of the building, and Avi watched the pair ride an elevator to their floor, walk down the hall and enter their room.

"Here comes Major Torsten now. He's going to spell me watching the cameras tonight."

"Excellent," Avi purred.

Alarm blossomed in Rebel's oh-so-expressive eyes. He liked making her a little nervous. If he didn't miss his guess, boredom would kill her interest in a man faster than just about anything else.

Avi moved his chair back to its position under the window. The hall door opened and he turned quickly. "Hey, Gun."

"Avi." A nod. "How's it going, Rebel?"

"All quiet on the western front."

"Great. You go get some sleep."

"Yes, sir," she said crisply.

"I'll walk you out," Avi said casually.

He followed Rebel into the hallway and closed the door behind her. They walked to the elevator in silence. Rebel was obviously as vividly aware as he was of the cameras Gunnar would be using to watch them.

"Walk with me?" he breathed without moving his lips as they reached the lobby. Gunnar no doubt read lips.

"Sure," Rebel uttered back, playing ventriloquist herself, and without so much as glancing in his direction.

It was a crisp Australian winter night under bright stars. The temperature was cool and bracing, perfect for a brisk walk. He matched his stride to Rebel's, relieved he didn't have to hold it back too much.

"So what's your answer, Rebel? Shall I show you how real men treat women? Yes or no?"

*Don't miss*
Special Forces: The Operator *by Cindy Dees,*
*available July 2019 wherever*
*Harlequin® Romantic Suspense books*
*and ebooks are sold.*

www.Harlequin.com

HRSEXP0619R

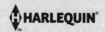
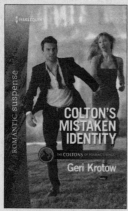

Need an adrenaline rush from nail-biting tales
(and irresistible males)?

Check out **Harlequin Intrigue**®,
**Harlequin**® **Romantic Suspense** and
**Love Inspired**® **Suspense** books!

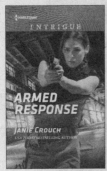

## New books available every month!

### CONNECT WITH US AT:

Facebook.com/groups/HarlequinConnection

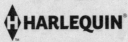 Facebook.com/HarlequinBooks

Twitter.com/HarlequinBooks

Instagram.com/HarlequinBooks

Pinterest.com/HarlequinBooks

ReaderService.com

**⊕ HARLEQUIN**®

**ROMANCE WHEN
YOU NEED IT**

SGENRE2018R

# *Love Harlequin romance?*

## DISCOVER.

Be the first to find out about promotions, news and exclusive content!

Facebook.com/HarlequinBooks

Twitter.com/HarlequinBooks

Instagram.com/HarlequinBooks

Pinterest.com/HarlequinBooks

ReaderService.com

## EXPLORE.

Sign up for the Harlequin e-newsletter and download a free book from any series at **TryHarlequin.com.**

## CONNECT.

Join our Harlequin community to share your thoughts and connect with other romance readers!
**Facebook.com/groups/HarlequinConnection**

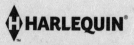

**HARLEQUIN®**

**ROMANCE WHEN
YOU NEED IT**

Earn points on your purchase of new Harlequin books from participating retailers.

Turn your points into **FREE BOOKS** of your choice!

Join for FREE today at **www.HarlequinMyRewards.com.**

Harlequin My Rewards is a free program (no fees) without any commitments or obligations.